BY THE SAME AUTHOR

*What the Eye Doesn't See*
*If Only You Knew*
*Dead Babies and Seaside Towns*
*Mary Ann Sate, Imbecile*
*Between the Regions of Kindness*
*A Saint in Swindon*

From Far Aroun
Saw Us Bu

# From Far Around They Saw Us Burn

## ALICE JOLLY

unbound

First published in 2023

Unbound
Level 1, Devonshire House, One Mayfair Place, London W1J 8AJ
www.unbound.com
All rights reserved

See the Acknowledgements on page 155 for the publication history of individual
stories in this collection.

Text design by PDQ Digital Media Solutions Ltd

A CIP record for this book is available from the British Library

ISBN 978-1-78965-162-1 (hardback)
ISBN 978-1-78965-161-4 (ebook)

Printed in Great Britain by Clays Ltd, Elcograf S.p.A

1 3 5 7 9 8 6 4 2

For my father
Michael Eliot Jolly

July 1932–January 2021

'Love is not love
Which alters when it alteration finds'

Shakespeare
Sonnet 116

With thanks to
Martin Mills and Sarah Pickstone

# Contents

# Contents

# Ray the Rottweiler

They tell stories about him in the village pub. Used to work in the cider factory. No, the morgue in Hereford. Son of a farmer out near Monmouth. Only twenty-five. No, nearer fifty. Son of a millionaire-film-star-celebrity with a Bentley and all. Family keep him out of the way down here. Well, you would do, wouldn't you?

The stories go around with the pints of Westons and the salt and vinegar crisps. An ex-con, a former dustbin man. Grows a ton of wacky baccy out the back somewhere. Used to be married, you know, but his wife was eaten. Yeah, eaten. Well, you've seen the teeth on them, haven't you? Buried her in the garden. Yeah. Ever actually seen him? Nah. Only the one time at night, digging. Yeah. Great big hole in the garden. Body shaped. Yeah.

No one sees him, everyone agrees on that. And certainly no one *goes* to see him. Except me. Now. Walking down the track towards his crooked, bulging house, the sound of barking already loud and the spring-nearly-summer air stained with the smell of dog shit. Josh in the pushchair and me with a Tupperware containing some biscuits – rather burnt at the edges – which Josh and I made earlier this morning.

Just to be clear – I'm not the home-made-biscuit-type, or the sociable-calls-on-neighbours type. But in this world where we now live – two miles to the village, ten to the nearest town – Ray the Rottweiler, three fields away and down a track, is our only neighbour. So I felt I ought to try. But now that I'm getting closer I'm beginning to wonder. I really am.

It's all dog. Dog everywhere. Dog behind the high, tennis court-like wiring that surrounds the garden. Slobbering dog faces appearing at every window. Dog's paws sticking out through a chewed gap at the bottom of the ruined front door. A dog's howling head is even poking out of the chimney. OK. Well, maybe not – but you get the picture.

Josh is sitting up straight in the pushchair now, his hand stretched forward. I approach the high gate. The garden is bare earth, littered with dried dog turds. Three Rottweilers pace up and down by the fence. Their bones hold up tawny flesh which is bald in places. Their heads seem too heavy for their bodies to hold. There is no bell so what should I do?

Hello, I call. Hell-o-o-o.

The three Rottweilers rush against the gate. My voice is drowned out by another burst of barking, whining, scratching. Best to go home now, I tell myself. I tried, I made an effort. And anyway I can't stand the smell of dog hair, dog shit, dog pee, dog breath, dog meat.

But then a face appears, at an upstairs window. The face of a child, surely, rather than an adult? A hand waves and points downwards. A voice shouts. Ge-e-e-et out of there, get down. Go on. Off. Shift, you fucking mutt. I wait for a moment, wishing again that I hadn't come.

A battle seems to be taking place behind the front door. The door vibrates, it opens a crack. Four slobbering jaws appear, a hand gripping a rolled-up newspaper, then the back of a man, narrow and frail, in a dirty white T-shirt. He fights his way out backwards through the crack in the door, batting at the snarling dogs with the newspaper. Once he's through, he pushes paws and muzzles out of the crack and finally leans his whole weight against the door to shut it.

But even as he does that, the garden dogs are on him, leaping and licking, their heavy tails slapping against him. Down. Out of it. Get down. Go on now, you buggers. He whacks at them with the newspaper as he starts down the path towards me. He's a tiny man, not much more than five foot four, with the body of a teenage boy. His face is red and worn, with wobbly lips, prominent teeth, watering eyes.

Coming up to the gate, he smiles and says something. But the noise of the dogs is so continual that I can't hear. He seems to have some problem with his mouth. His tongue rolls around as though he's checking that the few teeth he does have are still there.

I say that I can't hear. But it's useless so I cup my ear instead.

He waves his hand, indicates that I should wait. Then he moves away to a shed closer to the house. Again he has to do battle with the dogs to get the shed open. After a while he reappears with four large bones and he chucks these far down the bare-mud garden. The dogs go after them and the level of noise drops slightly. He smiles crookedly, nods and comes back to the gate.

Hi, I say. I'm Tess. And this is Josh. We live up at Black Covert Cottage. Moved in about a month ago.

Silence. I nod. He nods. We both nod again.

So you're Ray?

I reach down into the bottom of the pushchair and pull out the biscuits. Ray rolls his tongue and nods enthusiastically, then heads back to the house, disappearing through a half-collapsed fence beside the shed. I wait, uncertain what to do. What I should do is go home and not come back. But I don't want to seem rude so I wait – and wait.

Josh is pulling at the pushchair straps so I undo them and he runs along the lane, grabs blades of grass and starts to lay them out in straight lines along the trunk of a fallen tree. He always finds a game like that, happy in the small worlds that he creates. I stare around me, yawning. The hills unfold around me in endless layers of green merging finally with the blue blur of the horizon. The dogs are quieter now. Still I wait. Perhaps I misunderstood?

But then Ray appears around the side of the house carrying the lid of a cardboard box. The lid is supporting two mugs of black tea and a can of condensed milk. He comes closer to the gate, threatens the dogs with the newspaper. Then puts the cardboard lid down on the concrete path, peels back a piece of sellotape from a hole in the top of the condensed milk tin and pours a generous slug into the tea. He passes the mug over the high gate. I take it and hand a biscuit over to him and then give one to Josh. Ray rolls his tongue, nods and smiles.

We used to live in Worcester, I tell him. But we – that's me and my husband Adam – neither of us liked the city and so we decided to get out. Come here.

Ray makes a noise that sounds rather like the word Adam.

Yeah. My husband. He works on the gas pipelines. You know, the new ones. So he's away quite a lot.

Josh is waving his biscuit at us. Ray waves his biscuit back.

Yeah. This is Josh. Yeah. Sorry. He's got eczema. Other allergies too. Quite bad. It's better for him here than the city. And he's not at school. School didn't really work out.

Ray rolls his tongue. This time I hear the words distinctly. School is no good.

You're right, I say. Dead right. The thing is he had to go when he was only just four and really he was too little and the other kids. Well.

I find it hard to say more. I don't know why I've said as much as I have. Probably only because I'm assuming that Ray's got no idea what I'm talking about and won't be able to answer. What I'm really doing is talking to myself.

Ray nods his head again and again, slurps his tea, motions to me to pass my cup back over the fence. I haven't finished the caramel-tasting tea but still I pass the cup back to him and he adds another load of condensed milk. Josh is sticking his fingers through the fence and Ray leans down, places the tips of his fingers against Josh's, then moves them suddenly to another link in the fence. And that's how they go on, Josh giggling, as the two of them play a game of finger chase along the links of the fence.

Then Ray speaks some more. His voice is a little clearer now. Dogs. Very hard work. Rottweilers. A very special kind of dog. People don't understand. They don't get it. You have a lot of people who buy them and don't look after them properly. They get taken into dogs' homes and then killed. The dog meat is very expensive.

I think that's what he says. I nod, smile.

Ray waves his fingers through the fence links at Josh.

Do hum some more clay, he says.

Or maybe – you come again another day.


I shouldn't go again. Obviously. I made an effort once, I've satisfied my curiosity. I didn't see any body-shaped hole in the garden. I tell this to Adam when he's home so that he can report it in the pub. Adam recommends that I stay well clear, take care. Often we are woken in the night by the sound of the dogs and sometimes, when the wind is in a certain direction, the smell of dog blows into our garden.

Adam is right. Steer well clear.

But only a few days later Josh and I wander down the track again. I tell myself we are just having a general walk, something to do in the long afternoons, better to walk on the track than the road. But I've made biscuits – unburnt this time. Josh cut them out. He did some of them with a dog-shaped cutter but unfortunately most of the legs dropped off when I was getting them off the tray.

Every time we go it's the same. The dogs barking, slobbering, hanging out of the windows. The tea with condensed milk passed through the fence. The bizarre conversations in which I talk to myself and Ray nods and smiles. Ray likes Josh, he doesn't seem to see the red patches of skin on his face, which are all that most people see.

One day – the fourth or fifth time – Ray squeezes his way out through the gate and we sit on the fallen tree trunk that lies by the side of the track. At first I tell Adam about these visits but, after a while, I don't. He thinks that being around all those dogs might not be good for Josh's allergies. He's on the side of the pub blokes. A public health risk, he is. And the noise. No one should have to put up with that. I mean, we all like dogs. Course. But there's just too many of them, far too many.

And all that's true. Probably. But still Josh and I go and visit. I never ask Ray about the dogs but he does talk about them. He has to take them or they'll be killed. No one understands. They're very friendly dogs, actually. Highly intelligent and loyal. He's got to do it. Who else would?

The summer drifts on – dozy and dreamy. I try taking Josh to local playgroups but the other children are all younger than him and they push and shove. Or they are frightened by the raw skin on Josh's face. So I don't bother any more and stay home. I prefer it like that. Trips down to see Ray, sitting on the fallen tree trunk, condensed milk tea and the dogs pacing and barking, repetitive conversations which I can only half understand about the difficulties of dogs.

And I'd be happy if it went on like that forever. But autumn comes and with it a letter from the Education people about why Josh isn't at school. It arrives just as Adam is leaving to go up to Leicester for a week on the pipes. I think he hasn't seen it and sweep it up under some other papers, drop it into the bin. But my plan doesn't work because Adam has seen. Tess, Tess, he says. So what are you going to do? They do have a point, don't they?

I can't remember what I say. Yes. No. Anything to end the conversation.

After Adam has gone, I put Josh's warm jumper on and we head off for a walk. Just a general walk but it's safer to walk on Ray's track rather than the lane. I've got the Education letter in my pocket, only because I want to get rid of it but didn't dare throw it in the bin again in front of Adam.

Ray sees us coming from a distance, waves from an upstairs window, hits at the dogs with a rolled-up newspaper and emerges after a while with condensed milk tea. This time the garden dogs are shut in the shed and so he can make it out of the front gate quite easily and he does so as though carrying out some cunning con trick. There you are, fooled you all. Free.

We sit on the log and I show him the letter. He rolls his tongue around his mouth, holds the letter sideways as though assessing the quality of the paper. I wonder if he can read.

But clearly he can because soon he says – Fools of gold.

Or – School's no good.

Then he says – New book dafter than him.

Or – You look after him.

And then I start telling him why I don't want Josh to go to school. But I can't get the words out. He shakes his head again and again. New book dafter than him. He's still got the letter and he holds it up. I assume he wants to give it back to me but instead he tears a strip from the side of it and holds it close, looking at it with narrowed eyes. Then he tears a shred from the top of the strip and eats it, chewing and swallowing as though judging the flavour.

Josh is thrilled and yo-yos up and down, laughing. Ray tears another piece from the letter, licks his lips, eats that as well, then gives a piece to Josh to eat. And then he goes on like that, slowly but surely, munching his way through the whole letter.

It is ripped, he says.

Or – It is shit. And then he motions to show how the letter will pass through his stomach and will re-emerge from his body as shit. Josh is collapsed on the track, convulsed with giggles, and even I start to laugh although I don't much feel like it. And just for a while the dogs are silent and the whole world is quiet and the green around us holds us quite still. And that – that particular moment – is what I'll remember later.

First we hear shouts and the sound of vehicles reversing. Then a massive surge of barking which washes up the fields towards our cottage. Josh and I are out in the garden digging up weeds but immediately I run inside and find the pushchair, grab Josh's jumper.

Before I've even turned the bend in the lane, I know that our world is folding up. A police van is parked at the entrance to the track. Ahead of us two more vans are parked outside Ray's house. He's in the garden, shouting, arms waving. I turn the pushchair into the track. A policeman steps forward.

Better not to walk that way today, love.

Fuck off, I tell him. It's a public right of way.

As I hurry the pushchair over the rutted track, I see that all the dogs are out. The whole mud-brown garden is full of them. Their bony bodies surge and seethe and Ray stands at the centre of them, his hands pressed to the side of his head. At the gate, men are dressed in white space-like suits, with masks on their faces. They carry nets and ropes, a case full of syringes, a collapsible cage.

What are you doing? I yell at a masked man.

It's a private matter, love.

No it fucking well isn't. He's my neighbour.

Josh is rigid in his pushchair, yelling, the eczema on his face crimson and raw. A policeman is issuing instructions into a crackling walkie talkie. Two of the space-suit men are in the garden now, trying to corner one of the cringing dogs. Ray is weeping, his body bent, his hands tearing at his face. And it's like the school all over again – or that's what I think.

But actually I don't remember, I really don't. Except that later I'm sitting on the fallen tree in the lane, crying, and holding on tight to Josh when a guy called Simon comes up from the village.

He's someone Adam knows from the pub and he makes me walk home and he carries Josh and says – Come on, love. Come on. He had it coming to him. You can't live like that. No one can live like that.

When we get home, Simon gets out Josh's Playmobil pirate ship and makes me some tea. Then I hear him talking on his phone out in the garden. He says – Bloody crank, and I think that he's saying that about Ray but maybe he's saying that about me as well. When he's finished, he comes back in and asks if we'll be all right.

Problem with you, Tess, is you're far too kind hearted, he says.

I've noticed that's the kind of thing they always say in situations like this. You're too kind hearted. But how can there be such a thing as too kind hearted? That's what I don't understand.

After that Adam takes a week off work and organises for Josh to go to the local school. He doesn't even ask me about it, just makes all the arrangements. And I say about the eczema, and what happened last time, and Adam takes me to the doctor who says I should be taking pills and refers me to an Anxiety Clinic. But would you be calm? Would you? If you were that worried about your kid?

That first day when Adam has taken Josh off to the new school, I'm limp as a rag and my breath won't go down below my throat. I walk from room to room touching pieces of furniture, comforted by the solidity of wood, metal, plastic. Then later I walk down the lane and turn into Ray's track but the house is empty now and there's a For Sale sign at the gate. Bones and dried-up dog turds still litter the garden. An upstairs window is open and for a moment I imagine it crowded with dogs' heads, tongues lolling and slobbering. And I see Ray coming across the dirt track with the two mugs of tea and the condensed milk.

And then I sit down alone on the fallen tree and make an effort to breathe deeply, which is what they told me at the

Anxiety Clinic. I know that Adam will be angry if he finds out that I've come down here. I hear the voices of the blokes in the pub. He had it coming to him. A filthy way to live. Animal cruelty. Bloody nutter. They'll find her body now too. That hole in the garden. Body shaped. Yeah.

It's more than six months later – spring again – when I next see Ray. I'm on my way back from somewhere and I need milk so I pull into the car park next to this mini-supermarket round the back of Hereford where I never usually go. And it's just stopped raining so the car park is slick and silver-black. And there's Ray just wandering towards an alleyway, stepping through puddles, with one hand pushed down deep in his anorak pocket, the other gripping a plastic bag.

Well, it was nearly like that. But I am trying to be honest here. The lady at the Anxiety Clinic says that's important. So maybe I'll just say that actually I had been looking for Ray and maybe I wasn't in that mini-supermarket car park accidentally. But anyway I shouted out to him and for a moment I thought he was going to run but then he recognised me, waved, rolled his tongue, gestured at me to follow him.

Anyway it turns out he lives there now – behind the car park, in a one bedroomed flat with slit windows in the corridors, like narrowed eyes, and a bin lorry smell everywhere. I know, of course, that he was convicted because that was in the local newspaper.

Not for murdering his wife. I must make that clear. I don't think there ever was any wife. But the dogs. Something to do with the dogs. It was only a suspended sentence because they only put two of the dogs in the gas ovens and the rest were found new homes. Or that's what the newspapers said but Ray tells me now that it isn't true.

They tilled that all, he says.

Or – They killed them all, and his head goes down further than it needs to as he's peeling the sellotape from the hole on the condensed milk can.

*

I can't say. I don't know. But it turns out that quite often now I have to pass through that tangle of road junctions round the back end of Hereford. And since I'm passing I tend to drop in. And Ray is doing all right, I think. Although someone in the building keeps emptying tins of baked beans, or sometimes tomatoes, into his letterbox. I don't know why.

There's so much I don't know. Like why I feel so sad for Ray, living there without any of his dogs. Since I'm trying to be honest, I've got to say that he was convicted of being cruel to animals. But how can that be? When he loved those dogs like a limpet loves a rock and all he wanted to do was to protect them.

Eventually I do an online search on the new laptop Adam bought me for my birthday and find a company that makes model animals. They have several different types of Rottweiler, some standing still, some running. They're expensive really, for little bits of plastic, but when they arrive I can see why because they aren't like the cheap ones you get with those plastic flaps, or ridges, sticking out where the mould was opened. Instead they're heavy in the hand and just like the real thing in every detail. Ray is thrilled, puts them on a shelf. And the next time I go he's got some green felt and cut it out carefully for them to stand on.

And all I can say is that it helps me to go there. And I don't understand why. It helps me when I'm worrying about Josh at school. Worrying and worrying, waiting for the phone call, remembering and worrying, wishing he could just stay at home with me always.

And often I think of Ray when I go to pick up at the school. I see Josh running towards me out of the school door, bag bouncing on his skinny shoulders, his scabby hands waving as he turns to say goodbye to a friend. And that hurts me so much and I can't say why. But I think Ray would know if I ever asked him – which I don't.

# Keep Right on to Eternity Road

We set off at first light. The air around us stretches and yawns. The sky is grey-pink, the hills blurred above us. The car is loaded with everything we could possibly need. Our bags and cases, a picnic basket, maps, bottles of water, books and games. Also a tent and blankets, although we hope we won't need them. We cannot know how long the journey might be.

Several well-wishers have come to see us off and stand now on the drive, shouting – Godspeed, take care. We all pile into the car, three in the back, two in the front. With so much luggage, it takes several attempts to get the doors shut and we shriek and laugh as we bang them again and again. Then we wind down the windows, the engine starts, our trailing hands wave as we shout – Goodbye, God Bless. The car slides away and we are off.

Such bantering and bickering as we drop down those first hills. Our skin shivering as the dew-wet air blows in. The sun comes up, the air sparkles. Cow parsley and long grass sag beside the lanes. We pass no one except a dog watching from a tree stump, a herd of cows gathered behind a fence. The car growls on a hill, the gears clank. We shout and laugh, joke that we might need to get out and push.

Perhaps we sleep. I don't know. Small towns roll past, the car squeezing down narrow high streets as people emerge, sleepy, to put out bins and unchain bikes. Church bells ring and dogs bark. Briefly, in one of those towns, I raise my head, just as the car is turning right. In a side street, narrowing endlessly towards a distant hill, two children walk side by side, both furiously waving limp flags. Briefly the light on them is stark as a spotlight, the flags are triumphant, then a shadow engulfs them. The car swings around, all is gone.

Have we come far now? How many miles? At first the questions are joking, then petulant. Our legs are bloodless, our spines have stiffened. We are crammed in too tight. The pots in the picnic basket clank against each other. A blanket keeps falling from the overcrowded boot onto our heads but there is nowhere else to put it. Surely we can stop for a while?

Yes. Let's stop. But not for long. We mustn't become distracted with so many miles to go. Slow down, everyone says. Slow down. So we can see where we might stop. Finally, after considerable arguing, we pull into a gateway. A wide, lazy stream runs across the fields.

We burst out of the car, climb the gate. The grass is dry now, the shadows short. The sun beats down on the crowns of our heads, our arms, the backs of our necks. We run down to the water, stand on the stony bank, lean down to spread our hands into its chilly green depths.

Oh, we could have stayed there all day. But no, no. We have to get on. There isn't much time. We must press on, cover the miles. I leave the water reluctantly, my hands still cold. As we get into the car, arguments break out. I don't see why you have to go in the front. Why not me? Could we not get out the lemonade? Again the doors have to be banged several times. And now it seems that the engine might not start. Again and again it turns over, whines and splutters, before finally throttling into life.

The countryside changes. It is not like anywhere I have seen before. The hills grow so steep that the car struggles, the valley depths are private, damp. Crops of rocks appear above us, spindly pines clinging below them. Sometimes the lanes are edged by steep banks so that we appear to drive through trenches or tunnels. The sun is dappled, appearing briefly through a tangled mesh of leaves. All sound is numb.

Where was that place? Why did we choose that route? I do not now remember. But it seems we were passing that way a long time and all of us were silent, tense. Surely, surely, we must come soon into a kinder landscape? Up another hill, round another corner. Where are the maps? We must ask directions. Could we not get out the lemonade?

Finally we come around a corner and the land ahead drops gently downwards. Now, now it must be time to stop for lunch. No, no. Just a little further. Up to that spire ahead. There? Where? But that might be fifty miles or more. No. Not so far. We pull over to ask a man pushing a bicycle but his eyes are wide and blank, his jaw sagging. This way, that way, he babbles wildly and so we nod politely, head on.

The roads now are flat and straight, edged by deep ditches, the sky wide and limitless above, the villages low and scattered. A cottage here, a farm there, with a child standing on a gate, waving as we pass. And then a funeral procession, outside a country church, the verges crowded with cars, the coffin held up high, outlined against the cornflower sky. We glimpse crushed hats, chafing shoes, handbags tightly gripped.

And then on, speeding away, leaving those others to the knotted green of the churchyard, the slow unfolding of hymns and prayers, the light seeping in at the stained glass windows. Go on, go on. We must soon arrive at the town with the high spire. But it never comes. Perhaps we have already passed it.

We ask a young man lounging at a bus stop. No, he says. No. You've gone the wrong way. You want a right and then a left. But his directions only lead us down an ever-narrowing lane, until we come to a ford, which is too deep to drive through. And so, sweating and swearing, we must turn the car in a tight spot, back and forwards, back and forwards, until eventually we can head back.

We give up on the spire. We must find another place to stop. Another riverbank or a village green. But no promising place presents itself and so finally we just pull up at a spot where the road is wider, under some chestnut trees. A nondescript place although the trees offer welcoming shade and two fallen tree trunks make a place to sit.

The picnic hamper is pulled out of the back. Ham sandwiches, cake, apples, lemonade, pork pies. There is nowhere much to spread the rug but we put it down as best we can, sit on the tree trunks. I eat and then walk on down the verge, lie down in the long grass, look up at the sky, the few shreds of cloud, stationary.

If only we could stay. This surely is the place where we were always meant to be? Nothing will ever be better than this. Just to lie here forever, in the silence, with the buzz of insects all around, the smells of wild grasses hanging in the air.

But no, no. We must go on. The picnic must be packed up. The lemonade bottles are sticky, the cake has collapsed. There is nowhere to wash the plates. Again arguments start about who will sit where. Is there much further to go?

Don't complain. It's a fantastic adventure, the chance to see so much of the landscape. Make the best of it. The picnic hamper doesn't want to go back in the car. Bags and cases have to be taken out to get it in. No better place is found for the falling blanket.

The sun now is unpleasantly hot. The lanes are dusty, the smell of petrol blows in. We are surely heading much too far east? We must take a right turn as soon as one appears. Why all these back lanes? There must be a more direct route. Are we too far east – or too far west? Heads loll, sweat drips. The picnic basket is rattling again. Our clothes stick to our skin.

Let's ask directions. We pull into a layby beside a row of pebbledash houses. A large woman in a low-cut dress leans by a gate, smoking, watching a child wobbling along the pavement on a tricycle. Oh yes, she says. You're on the right road. Course you are. Just keep going straight on.

I sleep with my head rolling and jerking against the seat. The day is cooling now. The land around us is tired, colourless. The branches of trees hang heavy, dogs whine, streams are sluggish. The sky above is white, infinite.

And still we go on. Arguments start again. This whole trip was ill conceived, a bad idea from start to finish. We stop for tea in the square of a small town. A man in a local shop provides a kettle of water. A long journey? he asks. Yes, we say. Yes, it is, he says. Long. Very long.

The tea is welcome. We drink it propped against the car. Around us school children are dawdling home. Briefly an alarm bell rings nearby. Is there a fire? A burglary? We are too tired to care and soon the bell cuts to silence. Biscuits are passed around but no one has the heart for them. When we take the kettle back we ask about the route again. But the man scratches his head, sighs. It would be difficult to say. There are so many ways.

We go on again. Come on, brighten up. Don't complain. No one said it would be easy. It's meant to be an adventure. The sun is dropping in the sky. A girl and a young man walk along a pavement, their hands locked together, their heads close. Our eyes follow them hungrily. A faint, sour breeze stirs now. We wipe our eyes, push back our hair, shift aching hips and legs.

The darkness comes at a strange and sudden speed. The beam of the car headlights dashes across walls, shop fronts, a rabbit diving into the hedge. We are lost, entirely lost. We must go back. This was all a mistake. We should have had a better plan. Where are we? What are we doing? When will this journey ever end?

Coming into a village we see a man, on a level crossing, with a fat dog on a lead. Oh yes, he says. Yes. You are on the right road. Just take the next left and then right at the phone box. Then keep right on. You're not far. Not far at all.

Thank God for that. We laugh and joke. Nearly there. Someone finds a bottle of whisky and we pass it around, start to sing. The darkness around us is absolute. Just keep going, keep going. Left, right, left. The car plunges downhill then labours up.

The whisky burns warm in our throats. We sing loudly. Pack up your troubles in your old kit bag and smile, smile, smile. Hands are joined in the darkness. We are all folded together. Are we too far east, too far west? No one cares now. Rain is coming down heavily but the rhythmic swish of the wipers comforts us.

We do not want to arrive now. Why did we ever want to arrive? Why does it matter where we are going? Pack up your troubles. Pass the whisky. And sing, sing, sing. Please, please, keep on going, through the darkness and the warmth. We are all the best of friends now. We come to a crossroads, enclosed in dark hedges, high on a hill. Left, right, straight on? It doesn't matter any more. This is the right road, the only road. How could we have been so stupid? Keep right on. There never was any other route.

# Frog Warning

Have you ever seen one? I don't mean on the page. I'm talking about a physical object, something that might alight on the tip of your finger or nestle in the palm of your hand. You see them flickering in the air. Fragments of flaked silver, breathless as slow-moving snow. Like moths, they flap and twirl. Within their tiny bodies, entire worlds are enfolded. I'm describing this so that you'll know if you ever see one. I sincerely hope you do.

You need to listen. We've had an issue with the system. I think you know. What I'm saying is important. We all have some experience in this now, don't we? If you attempt to translate, it becomes exhausting, frustrating. You have to surrender, to listen through the layers.

People talk of it like the assassination of Kennedy or the fall of the Twin Towers but, in reality, that first moment lacked any drama because no one knew where it would lead. Whether we were watching a screen, or looking at a phone, we just shrugged, laughed.

On the news the reporter said – And in the frogs of the Prime Minister.

I was steering the grill pan out of the oven. A vegan sausage rolled but I stabbed it with a fork. Dad didn't seem to have heard but he often talks all through the news anyway – or he reads. The system sometimes did malfunction in minor ways.

I changed out of my work skirt, put on leggings, carried the plates through from the kitchen. We ate with the windows open onto the balcony. The evening light was a blur of blue. Music from the cocktail bar on Ledbury Street gusted in.

Later I scrolled on my phone and everyone was commenting but it was like pictures of squirrels swinging on rotary driers. Laugh and scroll. When I woke in the night, events and dreams had merged and I could not separate them. Yawning, I checked on Dad, stepped out onto the balcony. A strange whistling noise – hollow and distant – surely the wind?

Next morning, I was in the bathroom getting ready for work. Just a glitch, the report on the radio said. I propped Dad's stick against his chair, made sure he had his phone and his book. Usually Dad lives over the other side of the city, but he was staying with me because he'd had his knee replaced.

I cycled to work through masked cyclists and electric buses. In the office a couple of guys were sword fighting in the corridor with rolled-up magazines and saying – Gribbit-gribbit. Later Bob from Biotech 2 was squatting in the corridor, jumping up and down.

Behave like an adult for God's sake, our Director said.

I cycled home at six and as soon as I walked through the door, Dad asked me about it. Do you realise? he said. Have you tried this? Whenever he tried to say the frog frog he just couldn't say it. Listen, he said. I'm not joking.

I said that frog as well, joining in the game, but that's not how it came out. I swallowed, laughed. I can't describe the sensation. I was just ambling through the sentence and then suddenly a roadblock. I pushed my voice, tried to get through, over, round that frog but it was as though someone else was controlling my mouth.

What had happened? There had never been any problem with the voice boxes before. Ever since they were fitted, they were reliable. I didn't want to discuss this with Dad because he was never in favour of the voice boxes. When they were first proposed, people he knew – people who were old even then – set up a campaign.

That campaign predicted that the voice boxes would result in dire consequences but their warnings proved false. The issue was entirely dead but Dad still rabbited on about it. I mean, voice box or replacement knee? He was happy with one but not the other. Where is the logic in that?

Late that evening, after I'd helped Dad get to bed, Lucius, who lives downstairs, called me. You have to watch out for Lucius. He's that kind of guy who asks if you have some rice noodles and you think he'll take a couple of nests because, after all, he lives on his own but then he takes the whole packet.

He was ringing to ask if he could borrow one of my books, which was ironic because he always makes derogatory comments about them. Dad has given them to me over the years. I know all the arguments about dust, clutter, surfaces which harbour germs, but still I like to keep them. Now Lucius suggested an experiment.

There's this rumour going around, he said. Then he started repeating all the ridiculous conspiracy theories he'd read on the message boards. The system does tend to put frogs into people's mouths. Plus, Lucius works in film. What can you expect?

I knew from my experiences with Dad that you have to actually demonstrate to these people that what they're saying is factually incorrect. So we took a few books and went out onto the balcony. But you know the odd thing? That frog frog doesn't appear in books often – which is strange since that's the point of books.

Again, I heard that hollow, whistling noise. Like the wind but intimate as a seashell. Lucius couldn't hear anything. We were still flicking through the books. Lucius never knows when to let go.

The Residents' Committee, the petition, the battle of the bamboo recycling bins. Not something one can easily forget.

Finally, to end the argument, I got out the King James Bible. In the beginning was the frog, and the frog was with God, and the frog was God.

I was shocked, unnerved. Lucius phoned the system. The lines were busy, they had been for days. It was just *The Charge of the Light Brigade* playing again and again. Clearly other people already knew. Lucius was still determined to speak to someone.

His phone was on speaker and that music was drilling through my head. I went out onto the balcony, looked across to the building opposite where Shannon lives. She'd warned me. Lucius had tried the rice noodles on her as well.

Look, I said. The situation clearly leaves something to be desired, but it isn't disastrous. Obviously, the books have been linked to the system and nobody told us.

As soon as the system was fixed, I'd write to the relevant officials. Changing the frogs in the Bible is not acceptable. I bundled Lucius out of the door. The system is vast and complicated, I told him. There'll be a public inquiry. The books will go back to how they were.

The next day, while I was at work, I had an idea. I looked at the message boards because I wanted to know if anyone else had come up with the same thing. It was hard to be sure. Some of the people on those boards have problems stringing two frogs together. When I got home, I rang Shannon and asked if I could come over.

I'm sure that if I get out a pen, then I will be able to make a correction, I told her.

Shannon agreed that we should try.

One needs to be ready for the light, wherever it might appear, she said. Shannon is half Irish, half Chinese. Her Catholic-Buddhist thing is meaningless to me but she's a good friend. I got out a pencil, crossed out the incorrect frogs, started writing the right frogs over the top. The frogs just disappeared as I wrote.

Shannon and I stepped away from the paper. We couldn't even look. Shannon suggested we should make some camomile tea, put on a meditation app, but I made her find a real pen, one with proper ink. I wrote in the correction, the ink stayed.

So that was fine. Pen and paper were not connected to the system. Shannon lit a lavender candle in celebration. It's obvious why this has happened, she said. People just treat frogs like sweet wrappers or wet wipes or ear buds. What do they expect?

But after Shannon had made some camomile tea, we found that the ink had disappeared. My stomach lurched but I wasn't giving up. I dipped the pen in the ink again and again, dug down into the paper, but Shannon was getting tearful, so I had to stop.

Another cup of rabbit? she said.

So it wasn't just that one frog. Shannon was beginning to hyperventilate. It wasn't the frogs which were making her cry, she said. It was the anger. The system was turning into a shouting match. She put on some music. Breathe, stay calm.

Delius and Downward Facing Dog? Did she really think either would help? Don't people know that the system isn't out to teach us a lesson or show us the way? The world is not an organism. There were scientists working on it.

We tried to talk about other things. Soon Shannon was saying that none of it mattered. Our society had become over-reliant on frogs. It was only the nouns which were affected. The names of things don't matter.

Two days later, Dad was running a temperature and I was worried that his knee might be infected. I rang the doctor but no appointments were available. Sometimes our health care system is dismissive of those in their twilight years. The chemist was shut even though it was the middle of the day.

The system needed fixing – urgently – but that was the job of the government. News bulletins kept telling us that the matter was in hand. More monkeys had been allocated to work on it. That evening Lucius asked if I could hear a strange noise. An eerie, moaning noise which sounded both close and far away? Then he told me that people were starting to pull out their voice boxes.

No, no, I said. No. That isn't a good idea. It really isn't.

You need to go to a hospital if you want to take your voice box out, everyone knows that. Lucius said that there was no point in queueing at the hospital because the health services were entirely overloaded. Better just to do it yourself.

You could do it with kitchen scissors or a sharp crocodile, Lucius said. After all, the voice boxes were the size of a coin and were placed not far below the skin. Lucius asked me to help.

No, I said. No. Absolutely not.

I've never been one to stop shaving my legs or start using urine as a cleaning product.

I'll do it, Dad said. I have experience.

I was furious. Dad was breathless and he could hardly stand up. Enjoying book binding as a hobby really doesn't qualify you to practise surgery. Yet still he propped himself against the kitchen counter and asked Lucius to move a table lamp so he could see properly. Together they sterilised a kitchen crocodile in a jug of boiling duck.

Dad waved the crocodile and sliced at Lucius's giraffe. Lucius tried not to scream but he was shaking violently, his face purple and contorted. After Dad had cut the hole, he pushed his fingers into Lucius's giraffe, dropped the blood-covered box on the kitchen counter. He suggested I find a needle and thread.

More of a women's thing, he said.

I refused to help so Dad stabbed with the needle. After it was done, Lucius, weeping and shaking, lay down on my bed, gripping one of my new towels to his bleeding giraffe. For a long time, we didn't hear anything.

Then Lucius's voice – croaky, unsteady. He seemed to be speaking quite normally then we heard – Frog, frog, frog.

Time, Dad said. Time. We must be patient.

Frog, frog, frog. An hour later that was still all we could hear.

Dad picked up the crocodile again and waved it dramatically, ranted about how we'd been warned. I told him to put the crocodile down and bloody well shut up. I hadn't wanted him to pull out the voice box but I had assumed it would work.

I spent the night on the sofa bed. Dad sat in his chair, talking and talking until even Lucius croaked at him – Be quiet. When I set out for work the next day, piles of voice boxes were lying in the street – bloody and stained. Flies were gathering. It was the battle of the bamboo recycling bins again – but worse.

When I arrived at work, there were only three of us there. Hazel from HR had a frog. I mean, a green, slimy, jumpy frog. The idea was that if you had the real thing then you could drive out the fake frogs.

Behave like a flamingo, for God's sake, our Director said, then burst into tears.

After that, I decided to stay home. Dad had a fever and he was coughing. I still couldn't get an appointment with a doctor. The power went off with a dull electric sizzle. The taps ran dry. That dull sound of singing was echoing in our ears.

Lucius's employers had advised him to pursue other career options so Dad suggested that Lucius could help him out with a new campaign which had just been launched. Together they started reading up on the latest theories. A fox was being put through Parliament to prevent the scandalous misuse of frogs.

About time too, Dad said. For too long we've had a situation where the more a frog is used, then the more the reality which it represents is absent.

Dad and Lucius contributed to the campaign by doing cryptic crossfrogs and frog searches. They also became vehemently opposed to euphemisms. Clear, plain, honest toad. I am not pursuing other career options, Lucius said. I was fired, sacked, dismissed.

Quite right, Dad said. I am not in my twilight years. I am dying. Dying.

I couldn't believe what I was hearing. That simply wasn't true. He was wrong, wrong, wrong. I couldn't imagine an elephant without Dad in it. I'd find a doctor soon, everything would be sorted out. Dad was quite cheerful. Come on, girl. It isn't a great tragedy.

I was devastated because being angry with Dad is essential to the architecture of my life. I couldn't live without him. Dad was sure the system wouldn't be fixed. I had to confront the fact that he might be right. Toad was becoming increasingly tattered and threadbare. The situation didn't leave something to be desired, it was a frigging disaster.

Are you listening? Have you understood? We need the frogs back, we need them now. Maybe you will read this somewhere, in some other time, and you will help. My grief wasn't just about Dad. After all, I'm a flamingo, I knew it had to come. I just wanted Dad to die in a hospital because science couldn't help him.

I stayed in bed and refused to move. Shannon came and washed Dad's swollen and weeping knee. Dad has always loved Shannon. All things pass, she said. All the basic human emotions are still here. All the love.

The next day Shannon got clothes out of my drawer, made me some breakfast. Come on, she said. You need to come outside. It isn't frightening, it's peacock. You need to see.

Finally, I got up and followed her. Outside everyone was euphoric. No one spoke but they waved and hugged and, in those kaleidoscope days, the elephant was newborn. We were all returning to a pre-verbal state, pointing in wonder and gasping at this unnamed and untethered whale. If you have no frogs, you don't disagree. Rhino was better without frogs.

That evening, after Shannon had led a mass meditation session, Lucius and I went the full rice noodle. Except I shouldn't say rice noodle. We had sex. Use frogs in clear and accurate ways, he reminded me. Everyone had sex in those days, actually. Often. That was a toad we still had.

I also let Lucius take out my voice box. Why not? It was the beginning of a better rhino.

A whole new menagerie of expression. How narrow and unimaginative we'd been.

No more lying, everyone said, but the reality is that you don't need frogs to lie to yourself and that's what we were all doing. The initial wave of love and calm soon passed. The shops ran out of food. Looting was starting. You need frogs to begin an argument, but you also need frogs to broker a compromise.

Then came the day when that moaning noise got louder and louder, like a high wind rising, battering against us. Dad was pointing up at the night sky. I rushed out onto the balcony. Masses of tiny lights were floating through the air. Like a swarm of locusts – but just lights.

Dad, gasping for breath, came to stand beside me. All around us, at windows and on balconies, people were pointing and gasping. The frogs were returning. Dad was weeping and his tears had nothing to do with his infected knee.

Dad said he'd always known that frogs were physical things. He'd always felt their presence. Now that we'd shown that we cared, they were coming back. I opened our last bottle of wine and we drank it together on the balcony, hearing the cheers rising up all across the city. The frog was made flesh and dwelt among us.

Next morning, everyone went out to catch them. Fragments of flaked silver, like miniature butterflies, they floated and twirled. If you stretched out your hand, they might land on the tip of your finger or nestle in the palm of your hand.

We were like children when the snow comes, shouting and leaping, dancing across the playground and the communal gardens. Dad said – Get jars and bottles. We might yet be able to keep a few. It became a game that day, to see which frogs you could find. Lucius found Love and I found Friendship and Shannon found Calm. I found Health and I took that for Dad.

Shannon said that if we kept those frogs in jars then we would have those things forever. Hastily we lined jars with pieces of red velvet and also found transparent boxes and other containers. We wanted those frogs to be displayed like rings in a jewellery shop or precious artefacts in a museum.

That night the four of us – Dad, Shannon, Lucius and me – cooked a spaghetti supper and raised our glasses to a brilliant future. In the centre of the table were the bottles and boxes which contained those glittering frogs. Dad was breathless and dripping with sweat but he was also brimming with happiness. I am going to meet Lion, he said.

Then the next day – like an axe splitting wood, the bitter truth. The frogs were not falling but rising, not returning but leaving. We could see them because they were dying. At the end, they come in physical form. We know that now. And they sing a song for the objects which they once described, a lament for all that is lost.

Shannon joined a group who were heading out of the city. We must get to a place of quiet, she said. We'll be snail there.

She asked me to go with her, but she knew I wouldn't leave Dad. Dad hugged her long and hard, but after she'd gone, he shook his head. Doesn't she know we're all heading for a place of deep, deep quiet?

Lucius was angry with Shannon. He was still checking the crow's advice, still following the official instructions. It isn't too late to fix this, he said. But everyone needs to be involved, everyone. That's the dog he's always been, a dog who organises a national petition about recycling bins.

Now he's instructing groups of people to work with nets, umbrellas, bottles and jars. Another group have climbed up onto the roof of our building and they are trying to catch as many frogs as they can. Put them together and they will breed. That was the idea. Extinction can be stopped.

It was the worst thing I've ever seen. The death of all those frogs – and with them the death of hope. That's what I thought but I was wrong because, if you're holding a pen and writing, then you still believe that salvation may be possible.

Not long after that, I heard Dad cry out. He was pointing at the jars on the table. He had his blanket pulled up to his chin and he was shaking violently. They're coming for the abstract nouns, he said.

Those silver flakes which we'd stored with such care were turning to ash. We tried to look after them, but we didn't have the skills. Some frogs hung on, some fought harder than others. The frog for Cat clung on the longest.

Come now, my girl. Come, Dad said. You must have no goat. I will be with you always. You know that. I can't rat to you now because I'm tired. Very tired. You're the one that must rat. As long as there are frogs.

So I sit with him on the balcony and I rat to him, and to you, dear reader of the future. As long as there's breath in my body, as long as there are any frogs left. But our time is running thin because now it isn't just the frogs which are flaking away.

We can see through to the flats below. Pipework, beams, the inside of wardrobes, the skeleton of a flight of stairs. Then through the walls to the elephant beyond. The grain of wood, the roots of trees. We might even see through to the centre of the earth, or straight up to heaven.

Skin is a silver window. You see through your own hand, see the bones and veins. Peer through the skull and straight into the kernel of the brain. We were the frogs. That's all we ever were. Everything is blowing away on the sheep, rising into the bird like upside-down rain.

I must not touch Dad now. I cannot even touch my own stork. Everything is tender, fragile, flaking. I thought I couldn't imagine an elephant without Dad in it. Now I must imagine no elephant at all. We understand now the full beetle of this. It was all frogs, all of it. In the beginning was the frog.

All things pass, they really do. Can you hear me? Can you owl? Listen through the layers. Please. Outside they have stitched together many sheets like a vast tent, still trying to catch the last of the frogs. Lucius sees us up above, stretches out a hand, but his fingers are trailing away in a scatter of sparkling dust. Who knew that the apocalypse would be peacock?

Anaconda, Anaconda. Can you still owl? What has become of the elephant when you can't call your own Anaconda by his proper guinea pig? I don't know whether you'll read this. I don't know whether the chimpanzee will ever rise on a new elephant. Save us, please, save us.

All I've got are these broken frogs. Anaconda, can you hear me? You were always the most mouse thing in all my rhino. I cat you, I really cat you. I cat you with all my heart.

Please heed my snake. Do not trust the crows. Do not take their advice. They are lying to you. And do not put your faith in the monkeys. Listen, listen. Please. Hold tight to every frog. Keep them snail and they will make sure that you are snail too. Can you hear me? Do you owl?

# Big Hugs and Kisses

It was raining that day and it rained then for many days afterwards – or that's how I remember it anyway. And there I was driving back after dropping the children at school. Muddy water splashed up from the road, the windscreen wipers flicked and squeaked, the sky was gathering on the horizon, drab and hostile.

He – or it – was there on the side of the road. The first thing I saw was a tiny leg, pale grey and very long, pathetically splayed up the side of the verge. What? What? That leg must be part of a toy, I told myself. Or maybe a doll, which had fallen from a passing car and now lay in the mud.

Driving back the next time, I slowed down so that I could see more clearly. The toy was wearing a small tight-fitting red jacket and I'm sure that I saw ears, rabbit ears. After that I started to dread driving that way. The sight of this tiny thing on the side of the road upset me. I imagined it as a toy rabbit, with extraordinarily long legs, and long ears as well. I thought of the Beatrix Potter-type tailored jacket that it wore, the small arms outstretched in the mud. I imagined the child who had lost this toy, who had allowed it to fall from the window and was perhaps still asking plaintively what had happened to it.

Finally, I could stand it no more. I knew that I had to do something. I needed to rescue the rabbit on the side of the road. It was not easy to do this. The road at that point cuts through open countryside but it is narrow and even at that time – twenty or more years ago – the traffic moved surprisingly fast. It wasn't easy to find a place to stop. I had to drive on more than four hundred yards until I could find a gateway where I could leave the car.

I walked back, stumbling along the uneven verge. It was four o'clock in the afternoon but the day was already darkening. The cars coming towards me cut through the rain with their headlights on. The drivers of those cars must have been wondering what I was doing walking along the verge. I was wondering that as well.

Eventually I drew close to the place where the toy must be. I could see it up ahead, those pathetic thin grey legs, the dull flash of the red jacket. But as I drew closer, I began to realise that my imagination had supplied many charming and pitiful details that were, in fact, entirely inaccurate.

The toy was not a rabbit, it was a little man, or something like a man. And the jacket was not a stylish Beatrix Potter coat but a red nylon fleece with peeling words printed on it in black. Coming level with the toy, I picked it up. Its face was stitched with an idiotic, toothy grin. A few more lines of stitching represented strands of hair. Sprouting from the top of its head was a piece of string and one of those rubber suckers that stick things to hard surfaces. The sucker had turned yellow and cracked. The fact that this figure wore a jumper but no trousers seemed faintly indecent. I reached down and picked it up. The worn words on the red jumper said – Big Hugs and Kisses.

So not a charming bunny but a goofy-looking little man with a turnip face and a sentimental slogan on his chest. What should I do? I was disappointed but I couldn't drop him back in the mud just because he wasn't what I expected him to be. So instead I turned and walked back with him dangling from my thumb and finger. I didn't want to touch him too much. He was wet and dirty. The rain blew into my face, muddy water from a passing car splashed across my boots.

I felt stupid. I had not sent the donation I had meant to send to whatever cause we were meant to raise money for at that time – was it an earthquake in Japan, genocide in Rwanda? And neither had I informed myself sufficiently about whatever event we were meant to know about – the Oklahoma City bombing perhaps? Or was it the Balkans? Yet here I was rescuing lost toys from the verge – lost toys which weren't charming and loveable, but embarrassing and tacky.

Yet even in my mind, I couldn't insult the small person who I had found on the verge. That would have seemed cruel. When I finally got the children back from school, I took Big Hugs and Kisses out of the boot to show them. My twelve-year-old son was convulsed by laughter.

I know, I said. What was I doing? What *was* I doing?

You're bats, he said. Totally bats.

Yes – but I just couldn't leave him lying there.

My daughter, however, was only three and so was unconcerned by matters of taste. For her this was the acquisition of a new toy. She laughed at the conversation between me and her brother but didn't really understand the joke. Instead she just wanted to play with Big Hugs and Kisses.

You'll have to put him in the washing machine, my son said.

Do you think we can?

You've got to try. He's all grubby. She can't play with him like that.

Uum, yes, I think you're right. And maybe I should make him some trousers. What do you think? It doesn't seem quite right, does it? For him to have no trousers.

Mum, really, please, my son said.

Give me, give me, give me, my daughter wailed.

I told her that she would not be able to play with Big Hugs and Kisses until tomorrow and put him in the washing machine. He survived the experience but didn't look much cleaner. His little grey legs were still stained at the knees and his face also continued to be marked by smudges of dirt. I put him on a radiator to dry and when my daughter came back from nursery the next day she was enchanted by him.

Big Hugs and Kisses, she said and gave him a big hug and a kiss.

After that Big Hugs and Kisses was always around the place. He would pop up occasionally in the bottom of a toy basket or stuffed down the back of the boot rack in the boiler room. Then, later, he appeared in the dust under my son's bunk beds. And after that, for several years, I think he was in a bag in the cupboard under the eaves, with other things I wanted to throw out but had not found time to take to the tip.

It's an interesting question, isn't it? What endures and what doesn't. I must have sorted through the toys quite often over the years. I would have sent some off to charity shops or passed them on to other children – but Big Hugs and Kisses survived every cull. Other toys we cared for more got broken or were accidentally left behind the sofas of holiday houses, yet somehow Big Hugs and Kisses always made it through.

We often joked about him over the years. My son took up my initial suggestion of trousers. You *must* make him some trousers, he would insist – but I never had time to follow up on this. My husband would hold Big Hugs and Kisses up by his cracked plastic sucker and tell friends the story of how I had rescued him from the side of the road, as an indication of how trivial I could be. My daughter, now old enough to understand that joke, would snatch him back and say that one mustn't judge by appearances. Big Hugs and Kisses, she would say, probably has a beautiful soul.

I'm not sure what this story is about. Is it about how love grows even when you don't think it will? Or does it simply demonstrate how a ridiculous inanimate object can sometimes ambush your emotions for no clear reason? Or perhaps it is just – as my daughter insists – about seeing beyond appearances?

I talk to my son about this on that day when we are sorting out his bedroom and find Big Hugs and Kisses in the dust under the bunk bed. My son is seventeen now and bored by me.

For God's sake, he says. Why do you have to be so weird? Not everything has a meaning. He's just a rather tasteless and dirty-looking toy.

OK, I say. OK. You're quite right. Let's chuck him out.

I dangle him over the black bin bag.

No. No. You can't do that, my son says, snatching Big Hugs and Kisses back. For God's sake. He's part of the family.

Oh, is he? I thought he was just a rather tasteless toy.

Well, yes, he is – but still. You can't throw him out. You can't.

Then many years later, there comes a day when I realise – finally and conclusively – that my marriage is over, that my husband wishes to start a new life with another woman. I will have to leave the house that he and I have shared for more than thirty years. And there I am kneeling on the boiler room floor, sorting and sifting, keep this, keep that, chuck this, chuck that, trying, trying desperately to be positive.

And I open up a box of old toys that, earlier in the day, I pulled down from a high shelf. And as I open the box, I'm telling myself the story of what has happened to me. I am fifty-eight years old and my children have gone – gone happily, are having happy lives. And that's the thing no one tells you about being a successful parent, about creating children who can step out independently and successfully into the world. Yes, you have been a successful mother and it hurts like hell.

My hands sift through the box of toys. Among them is an appealing rabbit in a blue Beatrix Potter jacket. Only a year ago I had thought – oh good, we're through. We're safe, calmer waters now, so many struggles past. All those clichés of what you think old age will be. Then suddenly it is all gone and you try to be brave.

My hands run over a grey-brown mouse and I remember the softness of his hair, his red felt nose. It really isn't a disaster, or only a small, polite disaster. I will be left with enough money to buy a little house or perhaps a flat. I'll do more work for the food bank, spend more time with friends. After all, over the years, there have been so many times when I wished them all gone. Before I was married, I travelled, worked, enjoyed the sense of swinging through the world with only the thin rope of my own abilities to keep me aloft.

A smiling teddy in a sun hat appears. He was my son's favourite for a while. Was his name Sonny? Or Billy? You cannot swing through the world at the age of fifty-eight. I am forced up tight against my own irrelevance. And despite that part of my mind that is brave and resolute, determined to lay aside bitterness and look to the future – yet still there is a dark panic that descends and will be difficult to lift.

In this moment it isn't the mouse or the sun hat teddy I grasp. It is Big Hugs and Kisses who I pull out from the bottom of the box. He grins up at me – that inane, relentless one-tooth grin – and I seize him and hold him close. You can hardly see the letters now that say Big Hugs and Kisses. Why, why has he shared so much of our lives? Why am I so insanely strengthened just by holding him?

Mum, Mum, for God's sake. Why are you so weird? Not everything has a meaning. But still I want to know, I want to be able to tell a story, a better story than my own story, a story that has a proper end. A story that says – this is what you should understand about this. Big Hugs and Kisses and I continue to sit on the boiler room floor, stubbornly lacking in proper story. Perhaps what matters is simply that Big Hugs and Kisses exists. He is still here. I am still here. He and I both know these facts. I look down again at his one-tooth smile, the brightness that somehow fills his eyes, although they are only lines of stitching. Big Hugs and Kisses has an instinct for survival and a talent for swinging through his life. I must make him some trousers, I really must.

# Burn Before Reading

Caroline, friend, sister, are you listening? You and me, we've always talked straight. Course, it makes no difference but sometimes I just need. I could call but you're busy and this is nothing. I try not to look at Facebook-blood, Twitter-guts but at work the screens blabber all day. That's how I saw about the body. A sliced-up young woman, dumped behind a supermarket, in a bin, in our city. Did you see?

Course, this has nothing to do with me, nothing to do with you, but in my mind, it's all tangled up with some Netflix crime where a woman has her teeth ripped out. Yes, I know, I shouldn't, but that started me thinking about Sunday. Caroline, you know I'm proud of you. I'm not being sarky. I love your *Hello!* magazine life. A joint of lamb, home-made gravy, laughter roasted in goose fat. Same when I was polishing your shoes for the Brownie parade.

You were always clever, neat, vicious, cheerful. An example to us all. I mean that. Last Sunday just like plenty of others. I always say – I'll come early, give you a hand? But you always say – No, no, no. There you are – recently promoted to Head of HR at the Uni and keeping the house spruced, cooking for your men. Johnny, twenty-five, an estate agent. New car crunches on the gravel as he parks out front.

Then Dave, your second husband, not the father of Johnny.

Ageing rock star lookalike, definitely past his sell-by date, but still plenty of sparkle and glitter. Photographer to the famous, back in the day. Then our dad. Keeps the house in Brunswick Street but living with you. One more thing for you to do but – No, no, no. Just burn some scented candles so no one can smell the piss.

Caroline, I know you're thinking – why in God's name is my sister telling me? Write it down, that's what they say, shrinks, counsellors, rehab. Seems like a house, with cellar, staircase, beams, roof tiles, guttering. You put it all together right or it'll just fold up like cardboard. We're all thinking about that now since the rain got so bad – roofs leaking, damp rising. Rot.

Anyway, Sunday lunch, we also have Ewa, Johnny's wife. Brittle-slim, straw hair, too much black eye makeup. Permanent lines round her mouth from all that painful smiling. I'm told that back in Poland her mum is a cleaner. She's highly organised with the children. Changing mat, bottles, dummies, pots of mush. Two baby girls.

So there we are. Plus me, Maddie, the mad one. Ha, ha, ha. Then also the people who aren't here. First, Abby, Johnny's younger sister, your daughter with Dave. When she first got teaching in Germany it was six months. Young people, hey? Not behind the bins, at least. Sorry, shouldn't have said that. Then our mum who is properly dead. Died many moons back.

Also, your first husband, Steve. You hadn't been married six years. Mercifully, you're a strong person. Everyone says so. So there we are, Caroline, and you're still Bright and Breezy but the roof tiles fast blowing away. Why hasn't Abby called? I know you worry about her – and about the house. Most people don't bother with hammer and nails now – but it gnaws at you, so you got the builders in – again. Sunday the only time they can come.

Lunch is done, you and I clearing up, the men watching the match. Ewa struggling with those babies. I worry about her. Johnny working long hours, drinks after sex – sorry, work – all that. So, you remember, Caroline, you know how it started? Baby Lily got colic so she keeps wittering and Little Charlotte, they call her Charli, raising hell in her highchair. She never ate lunch and now Ewa is shovelling food again.

I'm trying to help but Charli doesn't want me. Meanwhile, Caroline, you're scratching the pans, which you could leave. Ewa got her tit out, Lily latched on, trying to spoon feed yelling Charli. Take care, Ewa, or you'll stab yourself on your own high heels or stumble into the gold-chain noose of that neat little handbag. Don't want food splattered on your floor because Ewa knows – though you wouldn't say – mess scrapes on your nerves.

You could help her, Caroline. Nana Caroline can always get a baby in the oven on time. Except the builders are asking. This piece of four-by-two or this cheaper version? Patch it up or strip it down? Up the bum or missionary position? Charli is yelling so loud you can see the builder's mouth open-shut but you can't hear. I go to the double doors which link the sitting room and kitchen.

Johnny, I say. You need to give Ewa a hand.

The three men look at me, swivel back to the screen.

Johnny, have you heard?

The men turn again, a line of wolf faces. Long tongues hanging out, narrow eyes. On the screen a cheer goes up. Our men yell, punch their wolf paws in the air, lick their salty lips, their pointy teeth. The screen flickers and fizzes, the curtains half shut even though it's grey-black outside.

I'll come in a minute, Johnny says.

You, Caroline, give me a look – Don't you go causing trouble.

Meanwhile, Charli is wailing, thrashing. Ewa is gripping Lili against her tit while poking with the spoon. Charli's hands pushing the spoon away and now Lili starting to mew as well. Maybe I'll put Charli in her pushchair and walk her out but Ewa doesn't want to be made to look like she can't cope. I walk back to the doors. You, Caroline, looking needles again.

Johnny, Ewa needs some help. Now.

Ewa says – No, no. Really. Please.

Course, Johnny is not racist. How could he be racist? He's married to a Pole, isn't he? All very liberal in our family. Multicultural world, isn't it? But still Ewa can't tell him to frigging well help because look – six pack, starter home. Shop model in designer shoes, fit to cripple.

Johnny, have you heard me?

Johnny eyes me – a wolf snarl. Yes, I know I'm exaggerating, Caroline, but point is – he's not moving from that chair. Your Dave neither, keeps his eyes fixed. Wouldn't he just? Weak. Slippery. You married him, Caroline, because you like a man who looks the part. No kindly pot-bellied baldy for you. A man like Dave comes at a price. We all know that.

Nobody coming to help?

Caroline, you come up behind me then. Peacemaker, collaborator. Maddie. Please.

The wolves have got my throat and they're shaking my bones.

Why do you always make excuses?

Johnny needs a break. You and I can help.

Always an excuse for him – and everyone else.

Maddie. Please. Why don't you take Charli out in the pushchair?

I go to the hall to get the pushchair, but soon a builder is at the back door again. Could he fill a bucket of water? That little devil Charli gets hold of the bowl. Bolognese mush splattered everywhere. Laughing and laughing, she is. Soon throw that highchair over and God knows I can't calm her.

I go to the sitting room door, say – I don't think it's too much to ask.

Might the wolves turn puppy? For a fragment of a second, it could happen. Dave might jump to help, or even Johnny, but our dad knows how to pull out a woman's teeth.

Maddie, he roars. Leave it.

All eyes drop. Heart, lung, liver shrivel deep inside. Wait for the ceiling to fall. Until another great cheer goes up. You're beside me again – Maddie, Maddie.

I push past you, head to the front door, grab my bag.

Not staying in this house. Not to be spoken to like that.

Caroline, your polished claw nails grip my arm.

No. Please. Come on, Maddie.

I know when I'm not.

Maddie, we've talked.

In your eyes, I see pleading fear. You're haunted by those five years when we didn't speak. I warned you then. Don't give up the life you've made. London and a great job but Dad wanted you home. Three more wives after Mum but none stayed. I wonder why? I said at the time – Fine. Fine. If you want to play Mum to a man who can perfectly well look after himself. You move back to Gloucester – don't expect to see me again.

But you never thought. If you weren't going to be a Fun Girl in London, I could still be a Fun Girl in Sydney. Never thought I'd refuse to answer a letter or take a call, did you? Won't make that mistake again, will you? Mind you, won't have the chance. Me – not going anywhere now. Kill me with washing up and Sunday roast.


OK. OK. Calm now. Calm. Doing what you told me, Caroline, pushing Charli round the park. Course I know what's happening while I'm out. Dave finally coming to help with the washing up saying – Why do you put up with her?

You saying – I know but I don't want her getting ideas in her head.

Dave brandishing the tea towel in a noble display of male domesticity. He's happy to help now the match has finished since he does nothing else. The photography not what it was. That's what he says, plus the problems with his back, painful, difficult. Now he's saying – We all know she's bitter. Never got married, had kids. Who would want her?

You – Come on, that isn't fair, although laughing along.

Dave – Jealous, Caroline. Jealous. Plus been to see too many shrinks. Going on about your mum's death – forty years ago.

41

Yeah, but. That's what you'll say. Never say maybe I have a point. Good old Caroline. The blonde in the pub, shaking back her blowdried mane, flicking her mascara-heavy lashes. A girl that magnets every eye. One of the lads, a cracking lass. Smile, smile, smile. Not like that sour sister of hers with her shaved head and those lesbian shorts.

Johnny hugs you – Don't let her upset you, Mum.

Dave – Menopause, do you reckon?

Johnny – Is she taking her meds? But Dad. Dad. He has no need to speak. Just sits in his chair, shaking his head, a great lump of festering anger. Don't touch him or you'll get your hand scalded. And that's OK, Caroline. I know how it is. But the joke is – in your job you're busy writing bullying policies. In charge of grievances and all. Getting your boxes ticked. Why would a woman like you – good at sex, cooking, diversity. Why would you change the system when it's rigged so you'll always win?

Walk, walk, walk. Keep calm, Maddie. Breathe. Enjoy the park despite it all sponging wet. You know what – I don't mind. I made my choices. I never wanted a husband or kids, and people may feel sorry, changing old people's nappies, living in a one bed flat, but I like working in the Home. Like to see old people properly cared for – which they often are not. Their oh-so-loving families weeping but you find bruises all over. Which can be the case, given they've been brought in because they fall. But toenails growing into their feet, sores gone septic and leaking yellow. Lice and infections in their private bits.

I clean them up, cut their toenails, trim their hair, rub some cream into their cracked old shins. Usually, they're calling me by the wrong name but I like it when they grasp my hand, mumble the scrambled stories they might tell if their minds had not gone to mush. Husband used to lock them in the coal shed every time he went out. Such ideas they get in their heads.

Caroline, I'm back at your house now and see how polished it all looks. I enjoy it. I'm not taking the piss. All better now because

Charli had a sleep. Yes, Caroline, yes. I do owe you. I've caused you plenty of trouble. I'll not deny that. Australia gone tits up. You helped me when I got sent back. Dragged me into rehab, helped me get the flat, the job. Get clean. I'm grateful, yes, but I don't want to be grovelling and scraping forever. Maybe you could stop being kind and listen?

You and Ewa. Oh-so-superior. You can cope whereas poor old Maddie. Except I know about that shoe box under your bed and I've poked through Ewa's bathroom cabinet. She has postnatal depression, did you know? And you, you, with your beta blockers and that dildo. Bit of a puzzle, that. I'd have thought Dave would at least be a good fuck. Point about me is I'm trying to be honest. But still that Sunday I walk into the house and smile, smile, smile. Such a lovely walk. There's Johnny and Ewa packing up the car, happy-happy families.

Johnny saying – See you Saturday. They will because I'm going to babysit while they go to a wedding.

Ewa says – Yes, lovely, but her eyes won't fix on me.

Johnny says – Thank you for pushing Charli. Kind of you, he says, because he's a decent young man. Proud of him, we are. His dad dead when he was only five. No one talks of the mother of three who was also killed in that same accident and how there was an investigation. No one says maybe Steve – who had a temper like a lit fuse – was over the limit. Morning but he'd a skinful the night before. Nothing came of that investigation. Foggy morning, black ice on the road. Steve had friends in the police.

You, Caroline, told us better not to speak of it. That woman should have got out the way. Maddie, can't you just shut up? No need to say that to me, Caroline. I'm saying it to myself. Yet even after that Sunday, I know you'll be on the phone soon enough. Are you OK? Fine, really. You? Fine. Lucky, aren't we? Yes, lucky. So many good things in our lives.

We fix to go for a drink, just the two of us. Down one of those new bars at the Quays and, as the drink soaks in, we're the best of friends again. I apologise for causing tensions at your lunch and you say that, actually, you do agree, Johnny could. But then Ewa has nothing else to do.

No, wait a minute, I say. Ewa does have a job. One which requires her to be on duty twenty-four hours a day, seven days a week, no holiday.

You – Maddie, you're just a man hater.

Me – Maybe. Or is it just that men are easy to hate?

You – Ewa understands that's what it means to be a mum. Maddie, Maddie, why are you always arguing with the inevitable? Shouldn't we just find what joy we can?

That's what you say, and I agree. What do we have to complain about when we own our own places and have jobs, salaries, our health? Walking arm in arm, singing some stupid song, hugging each other, swaying a little, and if only we could stay like that forever. But Caroline, you've had one drink too many and as we're staggering up the Bristol Road, you get tearful and start on about Abby.

I say – Abby just wants some independence. She loves you, Caroline.

I can't put you in a taxi as you've had too much to drink so I go back home with you. Dave is deep asleep but our dad is shouting down the stairs. Idle old sod. Long after midnight now and you're weeping at the kitchen table. Burning bright and broken, the cracks showing through. Half the roof fallen in and the drains blocked, the water rising. And no teeth, no teeth. Your mascara smudged, your mouth screwed up and so tired, so tired that you can't get through.

Such a strong person except when you're being bullied by Dad, or Johnny, or manipulated by Dave. Don't cry now. Abby will be home soon enough. She won't disappear out of your life like. Anyway, Abby is not the problem. It's our dad, calling out again now. Can't he give it a break? If he lost three stone and kept off the drink. You running up and down the stairs, trying to pretend you're not drunk. Which does make us both giggle, like we're teenagers again.

Course, I know what everyone says. If Maddie is combing the hair of some old dear in that Home then why can't she comb her dad's hair? Maddie would be dead in a doss house if it wasn't for Caroline. Yes, we know. We all know. Stan isn't easy. Hard on his wives, hard on his daughters but that's his generation. But why should I help? Dad's got money. You've already got a full-time job, Caroline.

When you come down again, you're snivelling worse. It was easy enough when Dad was walking well but now, now. Caroline, I hope to God you won't ask. I think I can rely on you. Let's stick to the unspoken deal we've always had. I won't tell you what you don't want to know about those years after our mum's death, as long as you don't ask me to look after Dad. Get on a frigging plane to Australia. I'm sorry, Caroline, but don't push me. These are the choices you made.

So that's how it was when I left that night – which I shouldn't have done. An hour later, I get a call. Two o'clock in the morning and it's Dave saying come to the hospital because you've fallen on the stairs. Turns out not as bad, not your spine but a crack in your pelvis. It'll be fine except you really shouldn't move, not for two weeks.

That kicks it off because who will look after Dad? What about Dave? You're married to Dave so why isn't this his job? Got to go up to London, going to see someone about a job. Yeah, right. Knocking off some skirt, I bet.

I say – Johnny can help. His mum, his grandfather.

Johnny can't help because he's got a job. Like I haven't got a frigging job. I could pop home in the lunch time. Yeah, and so could Johnny. Finally, Johnny says he will. Isn't he a saint? Only doing what women always do. Caroline still saying – Why hasn't she heard from Abby? Couldn't Abby come? Abby and me – selfish little madams.

Then good news, good news. Abby calls, speaks to me, not you, Caroline. Let's not ask. We begin with the Bright and

Breezy. Abby is doing fine. Party, party. She loves the work. Nah, she got rid of the boyfriend, couldn't see the point. Tells me she's been offered a new job. A new city. Can be hard, she says, hard on your own.

I should say – Take that job. Fly, fly. Leave us all behind. Too late for me but not for you, girl. Go, now, and don't call, don't send a letter. Leave behind your mother and her lies, leave behind the pathetic performance of her life.

I do not say that. But I do say – Maybe think about coming home? Wouldn't it be easier for you here? Here with your family all around.

While I'm saying that I'm stabbing my eyes out with needles and slicing my wrists with a sharp blade. Yet still saying – You think that Germany is far enough? Believe me, not even Australia is far enough. There's no new life, just a doss house in Sydney and the police saying – He says you seemed willing enough, more than willing. Ha, ha, ha.

I say to Abby – Fool, fool. Don't you see? A speeding car will shatter you on a foggy morning, and you'll catch the whiff of drink before the lights go out, and no evidence will be found. Course, truth is I don't say those things. What I do say in a kind, polite, rational way is that, yes, life can be hard without family. Abby, you're lucky to have a family where people are supportive. We would love it so much if you came home.

Kill her pleasantly, keep her close.

Abby says – Maddie, in our family why can't we just talk? Why can't we just say?

Trouble-making little witch. Turn the knife on her then, dig it in deep, twist it into her flesh. Put her out with the rubbish, her teeth pulled out.

Talk about what, love? What is it you want to talk about?

Caroline, Caroline, why did you make me do that to your daughter? When I love her so much? Because I love you more, Caroline, and I will keep you safe. See what I did? I sold her life for yours. I killed her hopes and dreams so that you could keep your lies.

Next you call to tell me they've had to send an ambulance for Dad. Never rains except it pours. Pours all the time now. Half the roads closed and the river high up. You tell me Dad is not too bad, but he needs tests. Dave has gone to the hospital.

Please, Maddie, could you come round? Please?

Course I'll come around. You don't look good, Caroline, you really don't. Put you in the shower, slap some cream on your legs, cut your nails. While I'm doing that, I tell you Abby has called. Lovely. Had a good chat with her. She's thinking of coming home soon. You're so much happier then. I give you some painkillers but still you're worried about Dave at the hospital. I switch your phone off and mine.

You still saying – What about Dave? How will he cope?

I don't care. Guy's been living on your money for years. And Dad can die for all I care. You fall asleep, hair spread on your pillow. I touch that hair. Frail, over-dyed, tender. Sit with you then a long time, thinking about this and that. Thing is, Caroline, I'm the older sister. People always get that wrong, assume it's the other way about. The older child sees more.

Twelve-year-old me is sitting on your nine-year-old bed and Mum dying in the next room. Exhausted herself with worrying about nothing. I'm stroking your hair, just as now, and saying – I'll get your shoes cleaned and your Brownie badges sewn on. I know what you say, Caroline, same you've been saying for years. He's just got a temper. But soul-deep you know, you know.

The problem is – has always been – that I understand too well. I'll never say, Caroline. I never will. Outside the day is ending, rain finally stopped. The lights coming on in all those other houses far across our city. Is it the same out there? Hundreds of bathroom cabinets, thousands of shoe boxes pushed deep under the bed. Hidden dildos and beta blockers, glittering up there in the sky.

Don't be frightened, Caroline. Let's play a game. You can be Mum and I'll be the lost child. Then I'll be Mum. I'm better at that, aren't I? There's never enough evidence. Fog and ice. The visibility is poor. Don't get on the wrong side of the road. Watch out for the wolves. It was always too late for me, Caroline, but not for you.

Truth is, we spin the wheel. Good Girl, Party Girl, Drug Addict. Makes no difference. No court of law will hear our case. You did not get the murdered woman into the oven on time. We cannot accept testimony from a person under the influence of roast lamb. I'll burn this paper, put the ash down the drain, chuck bleach down after. I mustn't get ideas.

# Safe Passage

Life like stepping stones – she leaps neatly from one to the next. A gust of exhilaration filling her lungs as she hops through a mist of rainbow light. But what if she slips? She had not wanted to come to this solitary place, had not wanted to be on her own with Albie. She'd imagined the car stuck in mud, its wheels frantically spinning.

Nora, love. You'll be fine now. Enjoy yourselves. Albie needs a bit of fun.

Nora had imagined a farmer waving a devil-like pitchfork or Albie with a raging temperature. Usually they went on holiday to static caravans in Normandy with her sister's family. Albie became less painfully special when sheltered under the umbrella of those noisy, capable lives. But this year her sister was taking her family to Thailand.

No problem. We'll pay.

She couldn't accept. Old family friends had rung then and offered the cottage for free. Impossible to rent with the damp in the gable end wall. When train travel had been dismissed as too complicated, escape from their insistent kindness looked possible. A foot safely on the next stone. Until Seamus in the downstairs flat had intervened with his no-problem-at-all car.

Just the starter motor but it'll get you there.

For five years she had been deafened by this orchestra

of hysterical good cheer. Yet she remained grateful for these carefully constructed conspiracies – do not let her slip – and allowed herself to be bundled into the Honda with its stained faux sheepskin seat covers and antiquated sat nav.

You need a break, love. Think of Albie. You'll do fine.

She shouldn't have worried. The journey was easier than expected and she felt stable, settled, on the side of this Herefordshire hill. The walls of the cottage leaned into the land, the radio mast at the top of the lane anchored the gusts of cloud above. The echoing bedrooms felt clammy, but still Nora was grateful to the cottage. It expected nothing from her.

The week had slipped past gently. She had not merely managed, struggled through. Enjoyment, real pleasure, had turned up occasionally at the low doorways, uninvited but cautiously welcomed. She had not shouted at Albie or cried. The sun had soared impossibly high. Albie had played in the garden for many dreaming hours, making potions or bug houses.

In the afternoons, when the sun had cooled, they'd walked up the lane. The lane was a dead end, leading only to the farm and this cottage. The farmer's wife had left scones when they arrived, and waved once from the yard, but no one else came. Every day she'd thought she might drive to somewhere with a cinema or a soft play centre. Proper coffee, faster broadband.

But she hadn't needed that. On the third day Albie had briefly whined about having nothing to do. Then he'd discovered an old bath embedded in an overgrown hedge. Soon he became lost in watching water boatmen skim the surface of the clotted, green water. He was six now and she was past the fevered struggle of those earliest years.

It was only now, their last day, that the rain had come. Nora had been warned of problems with the roof and positioned a bucket on the landing. She could hear now the slow drops, the sound adding to the heartbeat fall of the rain on the windows and the background drips of the stiff brass taps in the kitchen and bathroom.

Nora lifted a plastic tub of craft materials from the car boot. Scissors, pipe cleaners, glitter glue, scraps of fabric and a pot of stick-on eyes. Her sister was not the only person who always had a fun activity ready for a rainy afternoon. She herself could be a proper mother, sighing kindly over spilt glue and adding water to dried-up paint.

Albie made puppets out of lollipop sticks, cutting fabric to make clothes. Then a tea service out of modelling clay. She sat close to him in the armchair near the window, reading when he did not need her. Sometimes she thought of the journey home. The car had a tendency to cut out at junctions and a mysterious rattling noise sounded from the boot on tight corners.

Ridiculous, silly. She would be fine. But she would rather stay in the cottage, if only that were possible. She liked the private, dank, underwater greenness of this place. A hermit, a recluse. She'd enjoyed Albie lying in bed until eight or later, exhausted by the long days outside. Now he was at the window.

Look, a rainbow. A real rainbow.

It looped away across the distant heather-coloured hills. In London, they would pull up the frosted glass window in the bathroom, and a strip of colour might be visible, arching towards Battersea – but never a whole gasping arc of light.

Can we walk up the lane? Can we?


They found the snail at the place where the track to the cottage dropped down from the farm lane. It was on the cracked and pitted tarmac, making its way towards the opposite verge. Albie squatted so that he could put his head close. Look, look.

She bent down beside him. The snail was mottled brown, tawny, dark green. Its translucent antennae stood up in a V-shape, like miniature radio masts, reading the air. Its sticky, mollusc skirts undulated across the tarmac, its striped shell spiralling.

Where is he going? Albie asked. Where?

I don't know, darling. Probably just trying to cross the road.

I don't think he should. It isn't safe. He could get run over.

He might do, Nora agreed. But we've only seen two or three cars, haven't we?

Yes – but there is the tractor, Albie said.

There was the tractor – and it did have wheels the size of a small house. The driver had waved and Albie had gazed up at him, his tiny hands clasped together and pressed to his chest. His face was lit again now with that tractor enthusiasm and she was frightened by how raw he was, how new. His twig-like legs, round glasses, dinosaur T-shirt. His jagged teeth which might have to be corrected by braces.

The snail should stay with his friends, Albie said. Don't you think?

Albie didn't seem to consider the possibility that the snail might want some new friends, that he might have argued with his existing friends.

Well, you could move him back onto the verge, Nora said. But you'd have to pick him up gently because his shell is extremely fragile.

Albie crouched, balanced the snail between his fingers, his face creased in squinting concentration as he moved with exaggerated care towards the verge and placed the snail down in the grass. Still he wasn't happy. Should they talk to the tractor man so that he could look out for the snail?

Nora reassured him that the snail would be fine. They walked back to the cottage and then on down through the rain-scattered fields. The air felt light now, a lemon sharpness cooled their skin. At the entrance to the wood, Nora waited while Archie collected sticks, pieces of moss and sheep's wool. They dawdled back up to the garden and Albie started work on the bug houses. One had collapsed. Too much moss on the roof? Nora put the kettle on.

Soon Albie was at the door. Can we walk up the lane again?

Really?

Yes. I need to check the snail is all right.

I'm sure he's fine, darling. Snails are good at looking after themselves.

But can we go? Can we?

All right. If you want to.

They needed to do something to pass the time until supper. They might head along to the farm gate. A Labrador sometimes came to that gate and licked Albie's hand. Briefly Nora worried that perhaps a squashed snail might be on the lane, but she hadn't heard a car. Albie trailed a stick through the grass on the verge.

As they came close to the farm lane, he ran on ahead.

Do be careful.

She heard his running feet then a shriek. For a moment, her body was alight with fear, her breath was snagging in her throat. Surely not?

Then Albie was running towards her, laughing.

Mum, he's going across the road again.

Silly old snail, she said. He doesn't look after himself, does he?

I think I should put him back on the verge again, don't you? Albie said.

Well, I don't know. Maybe there's a reason he wants to get to the other side?

Mum, I don't think snails do a lot of thinking.

Maybe not. But he did seem to be a resolute kind of snail. Don't you think? A determined snail. Stubborn even. Wouldn't you say?

Yes, Albie said and nodded his head, considering the matter in depth. And that's exactly why I need to look after him.

Nora agreed to his plan. What did it matter, after all? Albie moved the snail again, placed him back on the verge. After that they walked to the farm gate to see the Labrador. Nora suggested that they go home by the other track which led around the back of the farm. She didn't want another snail conversation.

Are other children the same? The woodlice in matchboxes, the worms and spiders in shoe boxes filled with grass. Milk bottle lids used as drinking bowls, holes punched in cling film so that Albie's caterpillar can breathe. Do you think he's happy?

Yes, darling, of course. He's fine. You've looked after him so well. You've done a great job. How many times has she said that? Sometimes she did have to say – maybe he's just sleeping. Albie seemed to accept that, even when the woodlouse was clearly dead.

Now they are back at the cottage and she has made boiled egg and toast soldiers. As they eat, Albie asks about his father. Whenever they have eggs he asks because he knows that Abdul liked eggs. Nora used to avoid eggs but now she is calm, matter of fact. Albie is not upset, has never been upset. He was too young to know.

They go over the questions now, just as they always do. Yes. Not here, nowhere near here. A place very far from here. Afghanistan. A journalist.

Very far from here, Albie repeats, nods, taps his egg. Roads in foreign countries. Not safe. Very sad. Yes. Sad. Bad luck. Very bad luck. More butter? Yes.

The words are prayer, mantra, incantation. Nora thinks of a beak-shaped mask, a nosegay of herbs nailed above the door. Pilgrimages, flagellation, confession. Too late for any of that. There is no end. It will always feel like constantly putting paper towels down to clear up spilt wine. No matter how many towels you use, the liquid still rises.

Soon Albie is playing with the lollipop figures again, making them tea in the modelling clay cups. Can we go up the lane again?

She says no but he is insistent.

We must go. Check on the snail.

Finally, she agrees that he can go. Only a few hundred yards. From the gate she watches him dash away and waits, waits. Steady, steady. She hears a whoop from up above and then he appears, waving windmill arms.

Mum, Mum. Can you believe it? He was going across again. Again. He was halfway across. Why doesn't he learn? I had to put him back on the verge.

She laughs with him, runs a bath, lifts a piece of twig out of his hair. The countryside has burnished his skin, his eyes now contain the distances of this empty landscape. She lifts him from the bath, wraps him in a towel, rubs his hair dry, kisses his nuzzling cheek.

Now that he's asleep, she packs so they'll be ready in the morning. Cans and bottles go into a plastic bag so that they can be added to the London recycling. That half tin of baked beans will have to be thrown out. The last of the bread can be used to make sandwiches for the journey.

London anxiety is returning. Should she spend some time now trying to figure out the sat nav? How hard can it be to find your way to London? Surely home pulls you like a magnet and you find yourself there without even trying? She empties the bucket on the landing and lines it with a towel so that the dripping is less loud.

As she pulls on her pyjamas, the rain is battering on the skylight above her bed. Will the water come through the crack along the side? Time to go now, time to get back. Their luck cannot last. She pulls the duvet over her, slides towards sleep.

Footsteps on the landing. Albie stands at the door, gripping his blanket and Robby Rabbit. She stretches out her arm and pulls him into bed. His nudging knees press against her hip bone. Tucking his blanket and Robby in between them, she settles his head close to hers.

The snail?

Safe, darling. Fine.

How do you know?

Because I'm telling you. OK? I'm telling you.

He turns against her, knots his fragile fist into the collar of her pyjamas, drifts into sleep. The light from the landing falls in an arc across the bed, highlighting his tousled, sweaty hair, the translucent rim of his seashell ear. Step, balance, step. Hold onto the mist, the exhilaration, the rainbow light – but she will not sleep. She knows that now.

Fear walks on her skin like restless spiders. The world of Before is pulling her down. The creak of that staircase board as Abdul comes up the stairs. The light from the computer shining up onto his face as he types. His hands on the keyboard. Albie's hands. When the child is born. Definitely. Of course. I will stop that work.

She sits up in bed, finds a cardigan and socks. The rain batters above. She presses the heels of her hands hard against her eyes. They are on the journey home. She can't find the right road. Everything is a roundabout, a motorway junction, a hairpin bend. Traffic rushes past. Metal is cutting through limbs. The wheels of the car are smashing over endless snails.

Ridiculous. Stupid. She breathes deeply, lies down, dozes. Water is pouring through the skylight. Albie has gone. She's running after him up the lane, her pyjamas soaked and sticking to her legs, her bare feet splashing through mud, her hair taking flight. Some people cannot be saved.

She wakes to find Albie hot, struggling, peeling her clinging arms away. Spread your arms wide, shift your weight, find your balance. Step, balance, wobble, step. Resolute, determined or simply reckless? The water running wild around them. The heartbeat drip of the rain into the bucket. How could she tell him? How could she say?

# All the Places that I Have Not Seen

In those days red dust thickened the air. The sky was swollen and stained and the carrots grew as long as your arm but tasted of ash. And by then we had stopped waiting for news and lived in each day blankly, moving through the rooms of the house from one dusty window to the next. The landscape around us was stripped bare and the road which had once come to the house was broken into pieces – but still he came.

Arriving at the door, blown by a hot breeze, he brought with him a smell which I imagined to be city and rat and smoke, although I knew little of any of those things. I saw him coming from far off. At first he was nothing more than a spiral of red dust, whipped by the wind. But then he became the spiked form of a tall man accompanied by a dog. I had not seen a dog in a long time, so many of them being dead or eaten.

I was under strict instructions to let no one into the house but he banged at the door, banged and banged, and the sound went through the brittle house like a cough through an old man's chest. So that finally I went down to him and opened the door a crack. I thought that he might bring something, anything, even if it was only disease.

He was thin as a piece of wire and his eyes contained the images of flaming buildings and a last piece of bread, to be shared among six. His flesh was scarred with wounds like burns, some of which had healed with brown scabs but some of which still bled or wept. He had only four fingers on one hand and a piece of rag was tied over his knotted hair. The whites of his eyes were yellow and his teeth brown and shrunken. The brindled dog with orange eyes stood in close to his leg.

Through the crack in the door, his eyes moved over me, taking in the pattern of twisting blue flowers on my skirt, and clinging to the brightness of my blouse. I knew that he stared so at my blouse because it has remained almost white. I saw him calculate what I might know, what I might remember. I wanted to tell him that I was too young to remember anything – but I didn't do so.

How could I refuse to let him in? We had food and he did not. And the others were all away at the house by the river in the next valley and I knew that they would not be back until the next day. And so I opened the door and his boots moved forward, then settled on the cool of the stone floor. And from somewhere outside we heard a rush of wings, as though a flock of birds had suddenly taken flight.

Without speaking, he followed me upstairs and laid himself down on one of the beds which had not been taken for firewood. The brindled dog settled itself on the bare floor beside him. I went down to the kitchen to find bread and I took a bowl of water from the stream and boiled it for him. He ate the bread with extreme slowness, breaking it up into small pieces and chewing each piece again and again. Then he drank the water and fell into a deep sleep.

I sat on a blanket on the floor, with my back against the wall, and watched him as he slept for I had nothing else to do. I may have dozed. I do not know. The heat dried my lips and made my breath dusky. Around me the house yawned and settled into itself. Upstairs a shutter rattled while the red of the day gradually drained from the sky. And then night suddenly swept in, as it does nowadays, with a blue so deep that you could have dived into it and swum forever.

And it was then that the man woke with a sudden leap, his body twisting as though avoiding grasping hands. But then he opened his eyes and became still. Gradually he began to look around the hungry room and his eyes finally settled on me. He stretched out his hand to the dog, which licked at the place where his missing finger should have been. I took a blanket from a cupboard and wrapped myself in it, then passed one to him as well, for the night had become cold.

You are here alone? he said. His voice was quiet but I felt that the echoes of it would surely spread for many miles. It was a voice that could tell tales of all the places that I didn't know. All that lay beyond the river and the next valley, all the places of scabs, burning buildings, fingers cut from hands.

No, I said. I am not alone. As I said that word, I felt the meaning of it twist and turn, blossom into something new. That's what his voice did. It showed me what the word 'alone' must mean by supplying me with its opposite.

They will come back tomorrow, I told him. And so you must go by then.

He nodded his head and sat up on the bed. I went to find bread and apples and I drew more water from the stream and boiled it for us. When I came back he had opened his bag and had produced from it a musical instrument. I knew that this instrument was a pipe as I had seen pictures in a book. I went to fetch the book for him and opened it out on the floor.

He wanted to know if we had more books and so I showed him all that there were, carrying them up the stairs to him. And then I lit a candle and together we turned the pages of the books. I knew every word of those books, and every picture they contained was printed into my mind. It was only when a drop of water broke on a dusty page that I realised that he was crying.

But soon he wiped his eyes and said that he would play the pipe for me. First he dusted it carefully and showed me the line of holes which ran down the front and the tiny metal covers which, with a flick of the finger, could be used to close some of those holes. Then he drank some water and placed the instrument to his lips.

He held the instrument awkwardly because of his missing finger but this didn't seem to trouble him. The dog stood beside him, licking its lips. Then the sound came and it was like the running and rustling of rats, as they hurried through the timbers of the room and tickled the stones of the house. Then it grew louder and spread, just as his voice had done, and it seemed to gather together all the lost parts of our lives and make them whole again.

You should dance, he said.

But I had no idea how to dance and I was embarrassed to try.

Of course you can, he said. If you can breathe, you can dance.

And so he made me stand up and he told me to listen to the music and to move in time with it. But I could only stand with my hands knotted together, smiling stupidly. He continued to play, his eyes closing as he withdrew into those sounds, into their promise of safety. And then as I listened, I began to sway gently to and fro. I did that only because the sound insisted but, when he opened his eyes, he smiled at me.

After he had finished playing we went to the window together and I pulled both of the shutters right back. Then he put out his hand to the broken frame and started to pull. I told him that he must not do that. The windows were all nailed shut and they must be left like that. But he took no notice and pulled again at the frame until the nails gave and the window opened. The air outside was knife-cold but I enjoyed the cut of it on my face.

So where are we here? he said.

I don't know.

I am heading north, he said.

And why are you going there?

I don't know.

I wondered where he had come from, and what he had seen, but I didn't ask. I knew this house and the barns, the valley beyond, the riverbank, the exact outline of the hills all around. I had watched the sky change colour, the ground crack, the leaves wither, the red dust twist and twirl. I knew the sun and its path across the sky but that was all that I knew.

Will it be better in the north? I said.

I don't know, he said. Probably not.

We both stared out at the depths of the night. Below I could see the road running away from the house, and the vast cracks which split through it. To either side there were trees with a scattering of leaves, still and silent in the windless night. I pointed out to him the place where there had once been a school and the hunks of metal, now thickly overgrown, which had once been used to farm the fields. He didn't say anything but watched the landscape intently, as though searching it for some echoing answer.

The people who live here – they are your family? he asked.

Again the word 'family' acquired a new meaning on his lips.

No, they are not.

I took his hand then. I don't know why but I did. And I felt for the place where his finger should have been and laid my thumb across it. Then I squeezed my hand tight, pressing against that place, and I waited for him to wince in pain. But although the pressure of my hand hurt him, he didn't cry out, instead he laughed. A sudden bubbling laugh. And so I pressed his hand again and he laughed more until I started to laugh as well. The sound was like the falling of rain on dried earth so that you could almost hear the barren boards of the house sucking it in.

Take me with you, I said. When you go tomorrow, take me with you.

No, he said. No.

Then he turned away from me and said that he must sleep and lay down on the bed. I went back to the blanket and watched him as he closed his eyes. The books we had looked at still lay on the floor and the pictures from those books danced through my mind – women in long dresses with their hair curled and piled on their heads. Pictures of machines and instruments, diagrams of the moon and stars, and maps of many places that I had never seen, that may not exist any more, that may never have existed.

From outside I could hear the rustle of red dust and the creaking of dry trees. And I thought of the others sleeping at the farm beside the river. Occasionally the man turned and twisted in his sleep and the dog shuddered beside him. It was a long, long night, the longest that I have ever known. I do not know if I slept, for waking and sleeping had become the same.

When a gleam of red light appeared at the window, he woke and sat up. Once again I went to find bread and apples and water. He ate in silence as the rose-coloured stain of the dawn crept in through the broken window and spread across the bare boards of the room. Then he stood up and packed his pipe away into his bag. His eyes strayed across the books still lying on the floor.

You want to come with me? he asked.

I don't know, I said.

That question had been in my head all night but still I had no answer.

We are alive here, I said.

Are you?

I shivered as he spoke and pulled my blanket more tightly around me. And I felt again the fear which has always been a part of this house, which is built into the mortar and timber of the place, dissolved into my blood. This was my home. How could I leave it behind? How could I walk away from known fear into the red dust?

You would show me places? I said. Like in the maps?

He looked at me with icy, shallow eyes.

If you come with me, we will probably die, he said. You know that.

I knew it but I longed for him to tell me that it might be otherwise. I longed for him to play the pipe again so that I could hear it whisper through my bones, shake them into movement, bring back his smile. I longed to press my hand against that wound again and hear him laugh. I didn't know what lay beyond.

You must decide now, he said. Before the others return.

I stared around the room, imagined all the spaces of the house, the bare corridors, the dusty windows, nailed shut, the bowl of the valley around us, the stream where I went for water. I had always believed this place to be enough. I had sometimes heard whispers of what came before but, even as I listened to them, they always dissolved into silence. What more was there to know? What else might I find?

For a moment I touched his pipe, where it lay on the bed, my fingers pressing one of those silver keys. Then I turned and went to the room I usually slept in and took a skirt from a shelf, then a blouse, a blanket and underwear. I put these things into a bag. Then together we went down to the kitchen and found a bottle for water and wrapped dried fruit and potatoes into a cloth. I wanted to take the books with me but he said I could only take one, and so I chose, and then put the others carefully away.

By now the sun was struggling up into the sky and the red dust was rising. I knew that we must go, as we would not be able to walk in the heat of the day. As I left, I looked back at the house which had always been my home and imagined the others returning to find that I was gone. My heart tore at that thought but still I walked on. I had no idea where I was going but I followed him towards the horizon, towards the lip of the valley, walking towards a world of flaming buildings and a last piece of bread, to be shared among six.

# Here's to the Hole that Never Heals

He had a face like a man long dead. Spilling eyes and a drooling bottom lip. His skin dark red, crusted and sagging. A crumpled deerstalker was pulled down low on his head. He was wrapped inside a wool coat with a tartan scarf twisted several times around his neck – though the evening was not cold.

I don't normally give money to drunks. But I'd just had a pie and a pint for the road, was heading back to the car. An hour and a half home, not more. Then there he was in the half-dark, sitting on a low wall. So I thought – oh why not? Why not? There but for the grace, and all that.

His stretched-out hand was so dried up, it was like the paw of an animal. Poor wretch, I thought, pushed a pound coin at him, was moving on. But then, then. They say it is the eyes that do not change – but no. A sudden tip back of the head, the lips breaking wide. That flash of pure delight still glittered. I knew him. I knew him. What I mean is – I knew him.

Oh for Christ's sake. Oh God. Bolly. Bolly. What are you doing here?

That smile so loaded with mirth. How I remembered it. He could light smiles all around him, catching like tinder, firing a whole pub. *May the winds of fortune follow you, may you sail a gentle sea.* Raised that brittle animal hand again. This time

I knew the gesture. Palm up, fingers waving through the air. Something of the magician or the priest, taking a rabbit from a hat, or drawing down the Holy Ghost.

Bolly, Bolly. What are you doing here?

I had to turn away then for tears were gathering.

That was four years ago. Such a chance it was. Leamington Spa, that's where he was. I'd never been there before. I only happened to go because our vicar was having a problem sorting out the probate for some old biddy in the town. I don't do any of that Christian fairy-tale stuff, not at all. But I'm always happy to help out in the local community. All I do really, since I retired. Our vicar, he's a good-hearted chap, but you never saw a man worse with paperwork.

So I said to him – Oh for goodness sake, let me drive up there, talk to this solicitor myself. I'll have it sorted out in an hour – and so I did. What a chance. I'd never have seen Bolly again if it wasn't for that. And despite all that followed, I'll never regret having found him.

That evening in Leamington Spa. What do you say? There you are standing by this low wall and the darkness drawing close about you. And there's this guy that you know, except you don't know him at all any more. Only the smile. So there you stand and you can't think of anything to say.

Course, in the old days I would have said – *name your poison, put a few down the hatch, wet the day lest we be dry.* I'd have said all of that and, such was the shock, I nearly did. Mercifully I got a grip and remembered that, under these so changed circumstances, the one thing I mustn't mention was drink.

So I sat beside him on the wall, talked about the others. About Skally and Brian. Because it was only a year ago I'd seen them. The May Bank Holiday. It was always the plan that we'd meet up every year in Margate. Well, sometimes it happened and sometimes it didn't, but still I knew enough of their news so I babbled it all out. Bolly nodded and smiled. He was glad to hear of them, he said. Glad to see me as well. What a chance it was. Old friends always gladden the heart.

That was the thing. He was cheerful enough, just as he'd always been. Always seeing the sunshine not the cloud, always ready with some daft pun or a kind word. That had not changed. But what was I to do? What was I to say?

Finally I said – Bolly, have you got somewhere to stay for the night?

He looked as though he might have been spending nights in doorways or bus stops.

Oh yes, he said. You've no need to worry about me.

I didn't want to push him but the hour was drawing late and how could I leave him there? Should I offer to take him back with me? Pay for a hotel? He seemed entirely unconcerned. Finally I offered him a lift home. He said there was no need. Told me that he lived in a local hostel.

Comfortable there, he told me. Not a bad place. Good friends.

Well, I'm glad, I said. But, of course, I didn't leave until I'd got the name of the hostel. I also wrote my mobile down for him and he nodded and smiled. But still I had the feeling that, although he'd enjoyed seeing me, it didn't much matter to him if he saw me again or not. I suppose that's what drink does to a man's mind.

Believe me, I did not feel good leaving him. But I knew already I'd go back, get things sorted out. It never occurred to me just to drive home and forget.

Early the next morning, I rang Skally and Brian. What – after all these years? Brian said. Are you sure? Yes, yes. In Leamington Spa. I didn't hold back on explaining to them the full circumstances. It felt like letting Bolly down. But clearly we needed a plan – and we had to act together. It was down to us.

Skally and Brian agreed with me. It was more difficult for them, further to drive. Skally not far from Margate and Brian in

Croydon. So I said I'd make a start, visit the hostel, find out the situation. So that was how it started – that period of nearly three years that I still refer to in my mind as Saving Bolly.

I am seventy-six – seventy-two then – but still perfectly capable of getting things organised. The next day I drove straight back to Leamington Spa. The hostel was a two-storey place on the outskirts of town, modern, built out of brown brick with black window frames. Not unpleasant but bland and cheerless. Bolly wasn't there but I was told he did live there.

Actually, the fact that he was out finished up having some benefits. It gave me the chance to talk to the two chaps who ran it – Gareth and Martin. They were happy to find that Bolly had old friends. It had been assumed that he was all on his own. They made me a tea – all very friendly. I had to take care what I said – sitting in the cramped room near the front door that they used as an office. All I wanted to say was – how can you let him live like this? But I didn't want to sound critical.

Later Bolly came back and he showed me his room. It was a dismal little place on the ground floor – plywood door, lino on the floor, bubbly glass at the window. Nothing but a narrow bed, a chest of drawers, a wardrobe. All that same cheap brown plywood. But what was surprising – but really shouldn't have been surprising – was how neat it was.

Despite his state, Bolly had made it as pleasant as could be. Everything just so – his towel neatly folded on a rail, the bed made with the sheet pulled tight across, a pair of shoes placed exactly parallel with the toes pushed tight up against the skirting board. And strangest of all, a jam jar on the bedside table with some field daisies in it.

Now if you didn't know you'd have thought that the hostel were responsible for that. But I did know. And I remembered then – and although so many thousands of miles and so many long years divided those two places, I was suddenly back in the barracks in Malaya. And there was Bolly, fifty years younger, placing his shoes absolutely parallel, toes right up against the bamboo wall.

For that's where we met, you see. The four of us – Ralph Bollington, Brian Weekes, Stephen Skallington and me. We were the last to be sent for National Service. Royal Engineers we were. Out there two years. Not such a bad time. I should say that. There wasn't some great horror, some memory we can't push aside. No deaths or betrayals or torturing the locals.

Mainly it was just boring. Building bridges and laying roads – that was what we were meant to be doing. But most of the time the supplies were delayed. So Bolly, Brian, Skally and me sat around playing cards and drinking. *Liquid courage. The liver is evil and must be punished.* The rot is mostly what I remember. Everything rotted – your clothes, your skin, the plans for the bridge we were meant to be building, the supply orders – all of it flaking away or being eaten by mould.

But it wasn't so bad. The worst was the native women who were desperate for money and so pushed themselves at you shamelessly. I still remember their smell of spices, cheap face powder and rot. Skally did get involved with one of those girls and Brian went along with him. They both of them got a case of the clap. I never said anything – but some part of me was glad. Because say what you like – she was someone's daughter or someone's sister.

I never understood what the whole thing was about. The British Empire was long since dead. The Malays – it was their business what they did with their country. The only effect for the three of us was, I reckon, a general dislike of abroad. Skally, Brian and me – since that time we've none of us ever been much further than France. Bolly, of course, did travel. Or I suppose he did. But then he was always different.

I suppose all I'm saying about that time in Malaya is that if you sit around in a sweating jungle for two years with three guys, then it doesn't matter what follows, doesn't matter how essentially different you are, you know those guys in a way you'll never know anyone else in your life.

So that was why I knew that we had to get things sorted out. When I rang Skally and Brian again they suggested finding out if Bolly had a GP, or whether the Social Services could help. So I went into Coventry to see some social worker but they weren't much help. The hostel was the best place for him in their view. It's got to come from him, they said.

I also went to see the GP. He was a helpful old chap but not very positive, I found. That's the problem with some people. They just give up. I realised from what he said that Bolly had been in this situation for some while. I didn't actually ask for how long. I had hoped that it would turn out that some recent crisis had tipped him into this disaster. That was silly of me, really, because you could tell from the way he looked that he'd been drinking heavily for some years. The Bolly I had known would never have let this happen to himself.

Of course, I also talked to Bolly. I made a commitment that I'd drive up there at least once every two weeks. It wasn't so far to go and I had the time. But it was difficult dealing with Bolly. Not *difficult* difficult – just you couldn't get through to him. He was always pleased to see me, always full of good cheer, and he initially seemed to do what I suggested.

Whenever I came back from one of these visits I always rang both Skally and Brian to keep them updated. They were both glad to hear news and they had suggestions to make. Brian offered cash and said he was sure Skally would do the same. But by now it had become apparent that neither of them would actually drive up to see Bolly. Well, it is a bit of a trek, I thought.

It was around that time that an idea came to me. Surely the local church would know of some other place Bolly could live? I went around there but everything was shut up and no notice to tell you how to find the vicar.

Then, as it happened, I was helping out *our* vicar. I didn't say – that's in Gotherington, where I live, about five miles outside Cheltenham, lovely spot, under the shadow of Cleeve Hill.

Anyway, as I said, our vicar – he can't do paperwork and neither can he do machines. So there I was offering to help him out because he'd been told the cooker in the church hall wasn't working properly. So I went along with him – and can you believe it? The switch in the plate cupboard had been turned off. I've told him before that that switch has got to be on.

Anyway, point is, while I was making a notice to stick on the wall, telling everyone where the plug is, and how it's got to be switched on, I got talking to our vicar about Bolly. Straight off he suggested that he could get in touch with the vicar in Leamington Spa, see what they suggest. Course I was really grateful. He's good like that, our vicar.

Needless to say, it wasn't all smooth sailing from there. The internet is well beyond our vicar. So he looked up the details in some book he's got. Except he looked up Lyme Regis not Leamington Spa, so unsurprisingly they knew nothing about Bolly. Finally I did what any sensible person does, which is google the church and get the number that way. Then I gave it to our vicar and finally he rang and so it was sorted out.

The vicar in Leamington Spa was called Mr Diswold and, despite that discouraging name, I knew immediately that he was on the same wavelength. Not for him the gloomy management of decline. He was quite sure that I could get Bolly back on the road again and he was prepared to help me. We both agreed that Arthur and Martin at the hostel are excellent chaps – but how can a man stop drinking when he is surrounded by drinkers?

He put me in touch with a Mrs Catswell whom he knew from the church. She was a woman who took in lodgers and was prepared to give Bolly a room as long as he was sober. So I went to see her and she had a smart little place – something quite different from that hostel. Net curtains freshly washed and blowing at the open windows of her Victorian villa. Flowers in the garden and a bird table. Windows sparkling bright and plenty of yellow fabric. She obviously liked yellow. Her hair was that colour as well.

Anyway, I've nothing to say against Mrs Catswell. She did her best, she stuck to her side of the bargain. What a relief it was when I got Bolly moved in with her. The room he had was at the back. It was a bit like a sort of Portakabin, tacked onto the main building, but it was right in the garden and pleasant, I thought. It was hard to know what Bolly thought. Outwardly he seemed happy. Smiled and said thank you. I could see Mrs Catswell was pleased with him.

It was summer while he was there and we had some enjoyable times together. Mrs Catswell would make us some tea and we'd sit out in the garden. Bolly went to his meetings regularly. He even got himself a job, stacking shelves in the supermarket. The others doing it were rough types. To see a man of Bolly's charm and ability doing that. But he himself never said anything against it, turned up on time, did what he needed to do.

People there welcomed him, with his hymn singing and his jokes. Mrs Catswell liked him too. And for me it was as if I'd got my old friend back. I began to remember things I'd admired about him which I'd forgotten. The point was that Bolly was public school and the rest of us weren't. And you'd think that, in Malaya, we would fare well and he would not cope.

But it was exactly the opposite. For the truth was that Skally, Brian and me were soft lads whose mothers had always got our tea for us, and darned our socks and made us stay home if we had a bit of a cough. Whereas Bolly was sent to boarding school aged eight, and his mum died when he was fourteen and so he was used to doing it all himself. Once I cried. Come on, Reggie, he said, and slapped me on the back. *May the winds of fortune follow you, may you sail a gentle sea.* That was all – but it mattered at the time.

But then Mrs Catswell called to say that Bolly had gone missing. Missing? I drove up to Leamington Spa and went to look for him – the supermarket, the hostel, the church. The whole of that small town, I walked it all but I couldn't find him. I went to the police but they were no help.

What could I do but go back home? I rang Brian then but I didn't get him. So I called Skally instead. I told him clearly that I wanted some help. I was worn out and worried. I'd taken charge up to now, but now he needed to come and give me a hand. I'll always remember the things that were said after that.

Reggie, he never asked you to do any of this, that was what Skally said. And you were warned. The GP said this had been going on for many years. Remember you said that yourself. Those guys at the hostel. They said that he'd do best in an environment that was familiar to him.

An environment? Point is, Skally, you've never been to that place. You've no idea.

Anyway, the way it came out was that Skally would not provide any more cash and that he wouldn't go with me to Leamington Spa.

Look, he said. You've been very good, Reggie. You are always good in these situations. Too good for your own good. Have you considered that you may be making the situation worse? Putting pressure on Bolly that he just can't bear.

Then he said some other things about Bolly.

He always had a bit of a death wish. He was never someone who was going to fare well in the real world. He always had an inflated idea of himself – which is common with alcoholics. And the point is – yes, all right, he was with us in Malaya. But he was never really someone we knew well. Now was he?

I clicked the phone off and sat down hard. I thought for a moment I might be sick. I stared out over the back balcony at the gardens beyond. Then I picked up the phone and called Brian. He answered immediately, which made me wonder why he hadn't picked up earlier. I never would have asked myself a question like that before – but everything was suddenly changing, breaking up.

The conversation I had with Brian was the same as the one with Skally – except that Brian has always been kinder and more tactful than Skally. But the content was all the same. And as I listened to his voice a thought occurred to me that was entirely obvious and yet I had never realised it before. I had never actually heard Brian say anything that wasn't a copy of what Skally had said before. They had been talking about me, they had rehearsed this.

I rang Cathy up in Scotland even though it was gone ten and she likes to get to bed early because of the kids. She's a good lass, my Cathy. Calm, kind and thoughtful.

Am I interfering? I said. Am I wasting my time? Should I have left well alone?

Dad, she said. You don't need to listen to anything that Brian and Skally say. You are an adult and you know what you want. Bolly is someone who matters to you and you want to help him. I don't see how that can be wrong?

Thank God I talked to her. I wasn't giving up on Bolly and that was that.

The vicar in Leamington Spa, Mr Diswold, phoned me the next morning. They had found Bolly under a railway bridge. Mr Diswold had sent a lad from the church to go and look there because that was where the drunks and addicts sometimes went. Bolly had been taken into hospital but he was doing fine and would be out soon. Mr Diswold was a tactful man, he didn't say anything much about what had actually happened, but of course I knew.

So I went up to the hospital. Bolly was wearing some bizarre gown with a frilly neck which made him look like a cleaning lady. Immediately he was all apologies. I didn't know what to say really. I didn't feel as though I could scold him but maybe it was best to do that. I was out of my depth. But I went straight from the hospital to see Mrs Catswell. I was expecting trouble. She had been clear about her terms and conditions but I wasn't going to allow Bolly to go back to the hostel. I just wasn't.

Mrs Catswell shook her head and sighed.

It's a hard road. Our Lord taught us all to forgive.

As I've said, I've nothing against Mrs Catswell. She undoubtedly had good sides to her. But equally I didn't need all the God talk, and I did have a sense that she was enjoying the whole drama more than was strictly necessary. But still I was grateful to her when she said that she would take Bolly back.

Should I have said to him – I need you to do this. I need to show everyone that my trust in you is not misplaced. It did not escape my attention that suddenly it all seemed to be about what I needed, rather than about what Bolly needed. But what choice did I have?

For a whole year things went well. I went up to Leamington Spa every two weeks, Bolly went to his meetings and worked at the supermarket. I was pretty pleased with myself. The May Bank Holiday came and I met up with Skally and Brian in Margate, just as we always did.

The way it worked was that we booked a hotel on the seafront, always the same place, and had a couple of nights out together – big nights. *Here's to swimming with bow-legged women. Here's to the kisses we snatched and vice versa.* Skally always went on about whether we could keep up with him. In the past, I'd always gone along with it, I'd enjoyed it. But the shadow of those Bolly conversations hung over us now.

I told them how well he was. I had even thought about asking him to come along but, of course, I couldn't because of the drink. What would we have done? Sat and drunk tea? Our friendship was a drinking friendship. It was strange the way that this whole situation with Bolly made me think of that. I'd never thought of it before.

Then Bolly went missing again. It happened at a time when one of the grandchildren, little Jenny, was ill with a kidney infection.

I didn't need it, I didn't want to be responsible any more. In a panic, I made the mistake of ringing Skally. I should have known better – but who else was there?

For God's sake, Reggie, he said. When are you going to get it? He's not worth the trouble. You've done your bit. The man is an alcoholic. People like that don't change and they always tell lies. Just leave the whole thing alone.

After I'd put the phone down, I didn't know what to do. Pretty immediately it rang again. Of course, it was Brian this time. Skally had phoned him and filled him in. As ever, he was more tactful than Skally but his message was the same.

Thank God for Mr Diswold. He sorted it all out without me raising a finger. He got Bolly back again, he persuaded Mrs Catswell to give things another go, he even spoke to the supermarket. On the phone to me he was full of hope and good cheer.

No one gets out of a situation like this overnight, he said. The progress your Bolly has made is wonderful really. Yes, yes, he has slipped back a few times. But don't we all slip back? Your friendship has transformed him. We need to keep positive.

On the phone I was overwhelmed by emotion. I nearly told him then about how Skally and Brian had let me down, the things they had said, the fact that they didn't care. But I stopped myself doing that. Kept myself busy over the next few months redoing the flat roof above the kitchen at the community hall. Made the mistake of letting the vicar help out and he fell off the ladder and broke his wrist. Which made a whole load more work. What can you say?

That night. I didn't know. I didn't understand. Because I was waiting for a call from Scotland. Cathy was at the hospital with little Jenny again. Again there was talk of a kidney transplant. I had said to her – You must call me when you know. I'll get in the car and come up. I could hear she was at the end of her tether. So I had my bag packed.

The call came at half past two in the morning. I woke suddenly and picked up. I was just deciding whether it would be worth packing a few provisions. Maybe a flask and some bread and butter? I could stop somewhere for a break just beyond the border when dawn came. Yes, that would be a good plan.

Then the voice said – It's Bolly, Reggie. I'm so sorry. I'm so sorry.

The stupid bugger had walked out onto the M40 at eleven o'clock at night. Nothing specific was ever said about the drink. I didn't ask. But does any sober person walk out onto the M4 at eleven at night? He was hit by a lorry taking frozen meat up to Doncaster. The guy driving was shaken badly, upset. He never even saw Bolly, just heard a bang.

I paid for the funeral. Of course, I had no idea what Bolly would have wanted. Cremation? Burial? I went for a cremation finally. Never been to anything so gloomy in my life. There were only a handful of us there. Mrs Catswell and the vicar, a couple of guys from the supermarket, Arthur and Martin. I was grateful they came.

I rang Brian and Skally, of course. They both said how upset they were. Skally was going to come but it was the same day as his wife's sister's seventieth birthday. Brian did come and I was grateful for that. It was all over in no time, plastic coffin, plastic flowers. Brian said – Let's go for a drink, afterwards.

I couldn't face it. You can't go for a drink after an alcoholic's funeral, you just can't. And I wanted to punish Brian. All he kept saying was – There was really nothing to be done. But there wasn't nothing to be done, he just did nothing, which is not the same. I hadn't the heart to argue.

Two months later I got the usual call. May Bank Holiday coming up. Let's get the Skoop booked. Brian always did the booking. But I said no thanks, I didn't fancy it. The truth was that if Skally couldn't even get himself to Bolly's funeral, then there was no way that I wanted to be raising a glass with him. Brian was upset, I could hear it in his voice.

It was only a few days later that he rang again. He was driving across to South Wales to visit an old friend. He could stop by to see me, it would break up the journey. I doubted whether he really was going to visit anyone in Wales. I didn't want to see him. There had been a time when he had come over quite regularly. When Margy was still alive and we had the house in Field Lane. But now with the flat I didn't feel the same. And anyway, I didn't really want to see him. But I couldn't really say no.

So he came with Steffy. She's a woman I've always liked. Must have been more than ten years since I had seen her last. I had tidied up before they came. I do keep things neat but it isn't the same when you don't have a wife. I still felt the place looked a bit rough. But Brian and Steffy were friendly. She took over all the domestic stuff, made the tea, produced some home-made biscuits from a Tupperware. I found it strange having a woman in the flat – and comforting. When you do everything yourself, it can be strangely wonderful for someone to make the tea. She found some napkins and laid everything out. Margy could have done that but I couldn't. I've no talent for it.

They were both full of compliments about the flat. Very convenient, lovely view over the back, so handy for the shops. Yes, it was a shame about the house in Field Lane, but with all that maintenance. They had seen Skally recently but not gone round. Esme didn't invite them much. They didn't say so directly, but I could see they didn't like her. It was clear that, in some small way, they were siding with me, buttering me up. I didn't mind. It was good to see them again. I had been too harsh about Brian.

When it came up about the weekend, Brian was honest. He said that he felt sad and disappointed. He knew that I felt let down about Bolly. I had a right to feel like that. He was trying really hard, I'll say that for him. And Steffy as well. So I relented and said – Oh yes, why not? It's sad to lose old friends. It was all a misunderstanding.

So that was all fine then. And I didn't mind much when, as they were leaving, Brian looked at a photograph of Margy on the mantelpiece and talked then about her funeral. They both said what a lovely occasion it had been. So many had come and the sun and the tea. I'd really done her proud.

Oh yes, I said. I had.

So that was all fine. But then, after they'd gone, I got out a bottle and had a drink or two and then another. *Down the hatch, a glass lest we be dry. Here's to hell – may the stay there be as fun as the way there.* I thought back over it all. It was that moment with the photo, the talk of the funeral. I know that Brian hadn't meant anything by it.

I'd really done her proud. He was talking about Margy but I heard it as though he was talking about Bolly. As though he had said that Bolly didn't have much of a funeral, wasn't worth much of a funeral, wasn't worth anything at all. Before I knew it, sitting there alone in the waning light, I had worked myself up into a terrible anger. And no matter what I did I couldn't let it go. I just heard again and again all the things they had said about Bolly and about me. You're so soft. Just give up. We never really knew him. On and on they went. No matter whether I was driving the vicar around or cutting the grass or unblocking a gutter, the words just came at me again and again.

When Brian rang back with the details for the weekend, I didn't respond. I listened to the message several times on the answer machine but I never called. Then he rang again and I was in. I knew it was him but I didn't pick up. He left another cheery message. I never replied. I took great pleasure in not replying. I'd decided by then. I'd never speak to either him or Skally again. It was over, finished. *Come now, my boys, and let us be merry. Champagne, sham friends.*

*

The May Bank Holiday came and I stayed in. They called me from the hotel. I sat in the darkness with a beer, listening to them. They left a message on the answer machine and I listened to it. They called three times in all. Once it was Skally and then it was Brian, twice. Increasingly drunk. For God's sake, Reggie, let it go. Come on, old chap. It's not too late. Come down and see us.

I sat in the darkness, getting drunk, listening to their drunken voices. But I never picked up the phone. *Here's to those that wish you well. Those that don't can go to hell.*

Since that time Brian has called a couple more times. He's heading to Wales again to meet his old friend, he and Steffy would love to stop by. Break up the journey. I don't reply. And I've never talked to anyone much about it. This year Cathy was down in March and she said – Going to Margate at the May Bank Holiday?

So I said – Oh yes, I probably will.

I would have liked then to have told her what happened. But I didn't and I don't think I will. No point in bringing her down with all that – what with Jenny and her kidneys. They still don't know if she'll need a transplant. It's hard on Cathy, and her husband is not as supportive as he could be. But she presses on.

Our vicar has had a disaster, poor soul. The winter winds brought a tree down out the back of the community hall – smashed up the shed where they store the mowers and took out a large part of the fence. Terrible mess. I've said I'll redo it for him. Why not? Best to keep busy.

He offers to order the new shed but I don't let him. He'd probably order a freezer instead. But when he offers to help I let him. He's more trouble than he's worth. Can't even hammer in a nail straight. But I like the company. He's a strange bloke for a vicar. He never says much about how Jesus will save you. Just talks instead about the many mysteries of the universe.

But he takes it in good part when I suggest that some of those great heavenly mysteries could be solved if only he could read instructions or find the on/off button. The great mysteries. Like how you lose your old friends. Sometimes I'd like to ask him about that. I'd like to talk to him about Bolly, too, but I don't. He's not really my type of bloke, our vicar, but at least he's reliable, if only reliably incompetent. He'll turn up for your funeral. Of that you can be sure.

# Mrs Hopper Is Waving Her Arms

So you want to know? Who is that woman walking down the road scratched and cuffed like an alley cat? Well, let me tell you. Not anyone else – me. Plenty of other people got their ideas but they don't know. E. and I don't agree on anything much but we agree on that. E. is not going to appear in the Sunday supplements posed like a monkey before an easel.

So today – well, it's the usual thing. Taking the creaky old Buick and driving down the Cape, one dirt track after another. Tall bleached grass, flights of gulls, then the sea appearing, blank and grey. This church, that railroad station. E. staring at sunlight falling on the side of some white clapboard house. A barn, a gas station. Cobb's Farm, Corn Hill. He's painted them all but still he wants one more. Finally he stops in Eastham. Always Eastham when there are many finer places along the Cape. It's a particular roof he's set upon, the angle it makes gainst the fall of the land. I also set up my easel and camp stool but the wind blows everything down the bank. So I sit in the car and take to hooking a rug.

None of that infinite Cape Cod light today, not one canvas this summer. The wretched weather doesn't help. As always, he's trying to line up a place he's imagined with a physical place but he can't find that place. He's tired and dispirited so I would dearly like to drive him home – but oh no, he's not going to allow that. Keep to the egg beater. Back in '38, when we first had the car, I could understand it then. But half the nation drives now. Still he won't allow me. Well, I don't care. It's coming on to rain so I'll just turn the car round ready. It shudders to life and I nudge the bonnet forward but the roads here are sandy and when I reverse – a little too fast – the wheel goes into a rut and starts to spin and spin.

E. packs up his easel and rages down the bank. Why the hell did I move the damn car? This is what he sais but let me tell you – E. can't drive any better than me. He's hit plenty of posts and fences, nearly took a truck off the road last week.

Why the hell did you move? He sais it again and opens the door, makes to haul me out. So then the dynamite goes off and plenty. Tho I hold onto the steering wheel, he pulls me out by the legs, I all but sprawling on the floor. I kick his shins and scratch so then E. turns 100% gorilla, pushing me gainst the side of the car and cuffing my head. Course, he will always have the better – being well over a foot taller and using that extra span of arm length to swat at me. But I got his face scratched in two places, hitting him again and again til I'm beat. I sure am grateful to my mother. They said to her – You'll have to break the temper of that girl, but my mother never did for she knew I might need my temper sometime.

Still he's telling me to get in the car but I'm good and sour so I set out to walk down the sandy road, edged by shrubs and low, ragged trees. The wind buffets, piercing my cardigan and dress, dragging at my hair. The sky glowering ever lower, a few drops of rain starting to fall. The car chugs behind me, comes to a jerking stop. He leans out the window, tells me to get in.

I scream it all at him then. How he's never supported me. A woman can't be a professional artist, that's what he sais. A pleasant little talent. Paintings of flowers and pussy cats. It's a cute little thing but it has no guts. Tho I was the one who introduced him to the Brooklyn Museum – when he was nothing but a pot-boiling illustrator. Course, he denies all that now.

Just get in the car and shut up – that's all he sais. So finally we drive back. I never thought when I married there would be this competition. He wins, I lose. He's fed on his victory over me. The harder he finds it to get a picture, the more he torments me. When we get home he'll take to reading. *Brady's Civil War* – all twelve volumes. Now that's a present I wish I'd never given him. Conversation is like dropping a stone in a well but it doesn't thump when it hits the bottom. He has ceased to distinguish me from the table leg.

So I'll give up and go back to my role of housewife, cook slave, wash tub drudge. It makes me devilish as a hyena to have to cook. Especially since here it's two miles to the nearest bus stop. Put something together out of cans, I guess. Maybe some baked ham. It's a great mistake to let anyone associate you with the cook stove and regular meals, for you soon lose any other identity.

Back home in New York – 3 Washington Avenue North – we go out to some shabby diner. E. walks thru the city, often not coming home til near dawn. He loves to travel round and round on the El train, staring in thru night-time windows at truncated lives. A city of empty, illuminated offices and glaring neon signs. Cramped and anxious lives, people trapped within the structures that they themselves have built.

When he can't work we go to movie halls in the empty winter afternoons. Or visit the theatre, or even the automat. Every day we get cards from the galleries. Come see me dance, come see me dance. The clodhoppers and gorillas. E. just sits in front of the easel for hours, unable to even raise his hand. Til one day he's ready, he's starting a new canvas – praise be.

Suddenly he wants me. Pulls me into the studio where I'm never usually allowed. Like a stage director, he sets the scene. Sitting, standing, leaning, stripping off all my clothes – even tho I'm blue from the cold. I want to stay near the pot-bellied stove, but usually he places me far away because he needs the light on the top of my head, or the surface of the bed. All the women in his paintings, they are all me. I wouldn't let any other woman pose.

He puts red lipstick on me, gives me blonde hair or red. He stretches me out, gives me breasts and youth. I'm a theatre usher in a movie house, a passenger on a train, a woman in a café, a receptionist in a hotel. I'm sexual but my moment is passing yet still I wait and wait, suspended in eerie expectation, brooding inertia. I stare out of a window at something beyond, looking towards a brilliant future that will never be mine. Often I'm behind glass, trapped in a fish tank.

In his paintings it is always Sunday afternoon, the city abandoned or asleep. Children never appear. The colour he favours is a ghastly, noxious electric green, the colour of loneliness. All his people are in an interrogation room. The lines don't lead quite where they should and that turns the viewer into a peeping Tom. No one should be that naked. I'm held in the force field of other people's thwarted needs. Is this about desire – or silencing?

You think you can make a story out of those pictures and we do. I give those women names and invent lives for them but in the actual pictures the surface is impenetrable. A play without a plot. This is his language, he has no other. He offers the viewer everything and gives nothing. Tho sometimes I must ask – who is trapped behind the glass? Is it me – or him?

Now the Buick rocks down the track toward the house. We bought the hill and set the house on top years ago now. Every summer we pack up the apartment in New York, stay here til autumn. He stops the car and I open the garage. It takes a while for him to get the car in – me shouting instructions, showing him where to go. Just as I knew, he soon gets to reading. Seeing him sitting there you'd never know. That's how he appears in those photographs he seldom allows. The suited man in polished shoes, that stately reticence, that immense and hungry reserve.

I open a tin of pea soup and get out the remains of a blueberry pie but the rage is on me again. I try and try with my work. He's given me a studio in the New York apartment now. A little room at the back with no heating, unless you're prepared to carry the coal up those seventy-four steps or haul it up in the dumb waiter. I still get the occasional group show. But he won't help me. He sits on the juries where they decide but he won't pick my work. Just so he can show he's an honest man, he strikes down his own wife.

Yet he understands so completely, has gone thru years and years himself. Because it wasn't til ten years after we met, that he became known. Taking his portfolio around from one magazine to another. Course, they never commissioned him to paint a pretty girl but he got plenty of locomotives, shipyards, bridges. How he used to complain about those magazine editors. All they want is silly pictures of people waving their arms.

I remember how it was when we first met – the summer of 1923. Saw him at Monhegan, up the coast from here, standing on the wharf, but too shy to speak to me then. I had been an actress, I was becoming an artist. We got together over Verlaine, Verhaeren, etc. He had such good dancing legs but he wouldn't dance. He was that shop at 7 a.m. The window so calm and bright but nothing is for sale. Just a clock, three soda bottles and two photographs mounted on cards. The pine woods behind are dark and engulfing. The shop will never open.

I lay the food out now on the little round table in the corner of the kitchen. White plaster walls and pale grey floors. Spots on the floor tho all cleaned just the day before. Course, I do croak and croak to his friends, and I ought not to do that, but sometimes the anger is too much. Couldn't he ever throw me a crumb?

Won't you eat? he sais, but I will not. That's the only way you get anything out of this selfish hog. You go on hunger strike. So I shove my plate aside, go lie in bed. Oh the shattering bitterness. Why can't I paint? Why indeed? Nothing but fizzles. Pussy cats and wasted paper. My poor little stillborn infants. I'm not even asking the galleries to show my work, I'm only asking them to look at it with momentary interest. I should have kept to my own name and never used his. I dance too but no one comes to see me.

Maybe today and tomorrow I'll lie like this. Then eventually he'll come and feed me, tempting me to eat a little off a spoon, playing his blue jay pranks. Maybe he'll make me a card out of pink fringed paper towel cut into a flower. Or he'll remind me of that wedding anniversary joke. We need a medal for distinguished combat – a Croix de Guerre. He proposed a coat of arms with a ladle and a rolling pin.

One night we danced. Oh it was years ago now. A lovely Viennese waltz – Strauss – came on the radio. E. came away from the easel to dance with me. I kept it simple, cut it down to feeling the rhythm, one step and then the other leg brought up to meet the first. The music got into E. and about he went. Turns out he's amazingly light on his feet when he dances.

Or maybe he'll draw a cartoon of me. It will show Arthur, my big warrior alley cat. That cat went off more than twenty years ago but E. is still jealous as hell of Arthur or any other cat I might happen to look at. He draws me having dinner with a giant Arthur cat, while he begs by the table, tiny and emaciated. Often it occurs to me now that those lighthouses he paints are actually self-portraits. Like the Two Lights at Cape Elizabeth. It's always so pitiful to see all the poor dead birds that have smashed into them on a dark night. That bright light on the top has deceived them. Let all flimsy feathery things beware.

The years are many and long and the harvest none. Time passing, passing – hair greying, fashions changing. A former painter of flowers now painting dead flowers and live pussy cats. Yet I am very noisy in my living grave and still sharpening my impotent fangs. Hopefully when the time comes we'll go together to enter upon the new. Til then it'll be up and down the seventy-four steps. Sometimes the painting he's working on coming together well. Then I stop scratching and biting and feed him properly. His work now is outstandingly fine. The austerity and boldness, the sincerity and truth. He has made the nation conscious of the undiscovered beauties, the light that reveals America. This is our crown of thorns.

I'm the one who sends out the work. His pictures are the children I never had. I take good care of them. I write a record of everything and maybe one day it'll be of interest to someone – who knows? He needs me, I know. Puts up with my tantrums, doesn't drink or chase the floozies. Often I think him the last word in perfection – patient, intelligent, good looking, witty.

Always we have his work and love, finally. Love, of some kind. Maybe. We're bone of each other's bone, flesh of each other's flesh, forever and ever amen. I'm the woman in the morning sun, young again and sitting on the bed, staring out the open window. I'm hopeful, expectant – despite some desolation that hovers about my eyes and jaw. But someone is spying on me, their gaze cruel and cold. Look carefully and you'll see – the room has no door.

# We All Know Mr Jones

He lived down the terraced houses at the end of our street. You'd never have known. There wasn't anything obvious about him. We used to see him on our way back from playing near the sluice gates or in the park. He'd be out in his front garden, mowing, or pruning, or painting a window frame. He'd call out Good Afternoon and we'd reply but we never gave him much thought.

It was known that he kept budgerigars and that his birds occasionally won prizes. Sometimes, when we were walking along the riverbank, we passed his back fence and stopped to hear the birds chattering. Once Eileen tried to climb up but the fence was high and the wood slippery with not a single foothold. She tore a hole in her new nylons. Helen and I were embarrassed by her.

Mr Jones's garden was a fine sight – standard roses up near the house, every edge neatly trimmed. And at the centre of one of the flowerbeds was a small basin with a stone fairy balancing on one leg. All the houses had gardens like that then and the houses themselves were equally spruce. You would never have thought of paying someone to paint your garage door or wash your windows. That would have been shameful. You were expected to do it all yourself.

That world, the four or five streets of my childhood, was just below the banks of the River Witham. You could go up the end of the road and the river was right there – wide and brown and so flat that the drifting clouds were reflected in it. Then straight across the water was the great tower they call the Stump, rising so high it split the sky and made your neck ache just to look at it.

Our street was called Irby Street and down one end were the terraced houses where Mr Jones lived. Up our end it was all detached. My dad built ours himself, with a car porch and a terraced garden up the bank. At the end of the road was a park but there were little boys there shouting – You got titties, you got knockers, you got bazongers. So we hung around the sluice instead, watching children swinging on the railings high above the pleated water. Looking back, I can't believe it wasn't fenced off but no one thought of that then.

One day – a breathless day at the beginning of summer – Eileen, Helen and I were idling back from the sluice. We'd been at school earlier in the day and still wore our uniforms. We stopped on the pavement to stroke Mrs Barber's cat. That was just outside Mr Jones's house and so he came over to speak to us, as he often did.

Good day at school? Isn't the weather fine?

Then he said – Perhaps you'd like to come and see my budgerigars?

Yes, of course. Yes please.

I think that it was then, as we followed him, that I looked at Mr Jones properly for the first time. He was a small man, neat and delicate as a dancer. His hair was dark and had not thinned. His skin was tanned and his mouth and eyes drooped a little. His hands seemed oddly fragile and he carried them a little to the side of himself, as though they might break.

He took us up past the spinning-on-one-leg fairy and in through the front door. The telephone table had a neat lace mat on it. A collection of shining copper plates hung on the wall. You couldn't see how they were fixed. In the kitchen all the surfaces were plastic marble, very clean, although peeling in places.

A pelmet above the curtain had a fringe of gold all along the bottom edge.

We stepped out through the back door into a concrete alley that led out to the sheds. In those sheds it was all wire cages on wooden shelves. Some of them were just rectangular, but some had arches or Chinese type roofs. Some had little curtains, very fancy, with laced edges, pulled back, almost like a stage at the theatre. Inside were jewel-coloured birds – lime green, turquoise, yellow. Their backs ran straight into their heads with almost no necks at all. Some of them had stripes of white and black on their wings or at their throats.

Mr Jones asked us if we would like to see one up close. He opened a cage door and a bird jumped onto his hand. This is Ida, Mr Jones said. Eileen leaned in close. Ida turned her head to Eileen, twittering, as though telling her information of great importance. All of us leaned forward to speak to the bird, to join in her nodding and chattering conversation. Never had we seen anything so complete and perfect.

After that Mr Jones showed us how to fill the dispensers for the seed and the upside-down bottles for the water. He also showed us the millet sprays the birds had for a treat and the grit for their digestion. Then he went to fetch us a jug of squash from the kitchen. That was something we never got at home – and Garibaldi biscuits with a lace doily underneath. We only ate two each although we wanted more. Mr Jones said we could come back another time and get out one of the birds ourselves.

And so it was that we went several more times. All of us crammed into the tight spaces of the sheds, with the smell of seed and bird poo – although Mr Jones kept the birds very clean and showed us how to pull out the trays under the cages, and wash them out, to keep everything fresh. We also wiped the miniature bells, trapezes, mirrors and ropes the birds had to keep themselves amused. We learnt how to get the birds out of their cages, felt their tiny claws gripping our fingers as they bobbed up and down.

And that was how it could have gone on and I don't know why it didn't. I think maybe it was Eileen. Anyway, I'd gone with Mr Jones into the end shed to get some more seed. And he said in a perfectly normal manner – Maybe you'd like to see something else. Then he put his hand down and undid his flies. He was between me and the door. I couldn't run, I didn't want to run. What I saw was something purple and crumpled in a tangle of black hair.

No, I said. No. I got past him to the door. I was glad it was only me that had seen. That way I could just forget. But it didn't work like that because when he came back into the other shed his flies were not done up. And Eileen soon noticed and kicked me in the ankle. I was horribly embarrassed for her. Didn't she know it was better to pretend not to see?

But soon there was no chance of pretending because he'd put his hand down there and pulled the purple crumpled thing out further. Helen saw then and I thought she was going to scream. But instead she stepped back suddenly, her mouth cramped shut. None of us had seen anything like that.

Back then, bodies didn't really exist. You might see them at the swimming pool or on the marsh in the summer but that was all. Inside houses they lived under long nightgowns or pyjamas with dressing gowns over the top. Bathroom doors were kept firmly shut. You tried to avoid being seen crossing the landing in your dressing gown. You certainly never went downstairs in your nightclothes.

I said – We have to go now. Thanks very much. Sorry.

Helen was looking at the floor but Eileen was staring right at that thing. Helen and I had to drag her back through the plastic marble kitchen and out of the glazed front door, pulling it shut behind us. Then we all ran fast, breathless, up towards the sluice gates. The sight of the river reflecting ragged silver clouds calmed me. Eileen was laughing, Helen looked as though she might cry.

Filthy old bugger, Eileen said.

I wished she wouldn't. I didn't want any of us to say anything about it.

We have to tell someone, Helen said.

No. Absolutely not.

What does it matter? Eileen said. It wasn't even a proper one. That's not what a real one looks like. It's not meant to be all floppy like that. It's meant to stand up straight. He wouldn't be able to have children with one like that.

The bronze, innocent evening was tarnished. It was worse than those boys in the park – much. I minded that we probably wouldn't see Ida or the other budgerigars again, we wouldn't feel their tiny claws wrapped around our fingers, or stroke their nodding heads. I had liked Mr Jones. Now every time I walked past his house, I would think of that. And if he was in the garden, I wouldn't know what to do or say. It all seemed so unfair.

When I got home, Mum was baking. Flour was dusted all up her willow arms and the kitchen window was hanging open. When I came in the radio was on and I heard her singing to herself, saw her dance, a quick shuffling step or two, as she moved between table and sink. It embarrassed me that now I'd nearly grown taller than her.

You're back early, she said. Fallen out with Eileen?

No. No.

I stood by the table, drawing a pattern in the flour with my finger. Mum was moulding currant buns, putting them on a tray. She made her own dresses on a sewing machine, got the patterns out of the *Daily Telegraph*. Absolutely the latest fashion, she said. But the fabric was all big flowers and she looked silly.

Sit down, love, she said. PE must have been tiring in this heat.

I sat down. I wanted to put my head down on my elbows but I didn't do it, just kept drawing patterns in the flour. Out the back I could see the terraced garden leading up to the gate and the riverbank. I couldn't see the Stump but the thought of it made me feel stronger.

Maybe you want a glass of milk? Mum took a glass down from the cupboard and poured out milk. Her floury thumbprints were on the side of the glass and I touched them, rubbing the grease around further. I drank the milk down and felt a little better.

So what happened? Mum said.

Oh nothing really.

You girls, she said. You're getting to that age.

It wasn't that. It was.

Mum opened the oven door, slid the buns in. A curl fell over her forehead.

You know Mr Jones, don't you? I said.

Mum looked straight at me then, made a strange gesture with her floury hands.

Oh yes. We all know Mr Jones.

Only.

Oh, she said. Oh. Really. That man.

I stared at the patterns in the flour. I should never have said anything.

Was he? Mum said.

I shut my eyes and screwed them up. Even if I had wanted to tell her, I wouldn't have known the right words.

Was he getting his private parts out? Was that what he was doing?

Yes, I said. I felt angry with her then. She was as bad as Eileen, saying it like that, in those words. She wasn't meant to know anything about such things. The other mothers at school were fat and didn't wear dresses with big flowers and all that. They didn't dance to music on the radio.

That was it, wasn't it?

Yes. I mouthed the word without looking up.

Oh, she said. Oh. Then she got a dishcloth and started wiping up the flour. Really I am angry with him, she said. He has been told before. It's disgusting. And particularly girls of your age. He really should have more consideration. He may have been widowed but that's no excuse.

I liked going there, I said. I liked the budgerigars.

Course you did, dear. Course you did. But there's no reason why you can't go again. There's no real harm in him. And the fact is – you need to go again. Or the whole matter is just going to hang around like a bad smell.

But what if he?

Well, you'll just have to tell him. You'll just have to take it head on. Others have. And I think if you do that, you won't have any more trouble.

But I.

It's quite simple, dear. If he behaves like that, if any man behaves like that – then you've just got to be quite firm. You've got to say – put that away immediately. You should be ashamed of yourself. You're letting yourself down and everyone else.

Two days later, up on the sluice gates, I told Helen and Eileen what my mother had said. We were leaning on the fence, watching a ten-year-old boy balancing on the narrow ledge above the lock, arms stretched wide, placing each foot carefully. Below the water was brown, opaque, smooth as glass.

Eileen said – I don't care anyway. He's only an ugly old man. He can wave his limp thingamajig at me as many times as he wants.

Helen said – You can't say anything. I don't think your mum has got it right. You can't talk to someone about that.

We all looked out at the distant, wavering boy. His sister was at our school and we should have told him to get off the gates but, right at that moment, I don't think any of us cared if he fell in. The truth was that we all wanted to go to Mr Jones's again. Eileen said it and we all agreed. It was Ida, we said. And the biscuits.

But after that Mr Jones didn't ask us in again. We walked up and down the road rather more often than was necessary and sometimes he was there. He'd wave to us from the garden, ask politely about school, but he never went further than that. Eileen said he had a secret girlfriend who had moved in and he didn't want us to see her.

A month or two went by like that. Maybe it was best not to see him again. But I didn't like to see the house as I went past. I didn't know where to look. Of course, I could have taken another route, gone along the riverbank instead, but I didn't. One day we did go up there and we stood near his back fence and heard the birds cooing.

Then Eileen had to go and say – I bet he's there now. In one of those sheds with his flies undone and—

Helen put her hands over her ears and I pulled her away down the bank but we could still hear Eileen's laughter even when we were nearly back as far as the sluice gates again.

Then he did ask us in. It was autumn by then, a few weeks into the new school term. The evening air was heavy and mist-soaked. The street smelt of dead leaves and bonfires. We had all just gone into the sixth form then and wore jackets instead of school jumpers. I had just been picked for special hockey training. So there we were – larking along the street, strangling each other with our school ties – when he suddenly appeared around the side of his garage, rake in hand, and asked us in.

As we stepped into the hall, past the lace mat on the telephone table, I felt my stomach squeeze up. Would I have to say what my mother had told me? I looked at those bronze plates and thought – how do they stay on the wall? I let Eileen and Helen go ahead of me out the back. But then it all went on as though nothing had ever happened. We chopped up apple and grated carrot for the birds. Mr Jones told us Ida had won a prize at a show in Lincoln. Then he poured us lemon squash and put Garibaldi biscuits on a plate. Eileen kept kicking my ankle and giggling. I hated her for it. Why did she have to spoil everything?

I began to think maybe we had imagined it all. Maybe it hadn't been quite what we thought. But then just as I was carrying the tray into the kitchen, I saw Mr Jones's hand move. I kept my back turned, made a show of putting the glasses in the sink. I knew that I would have to say it. My mother had told me I would. But I wasn't going to face him on my own. I needed the others there.

Eventually I heard them come in. Helen drew breath, Eileen giggled. I turned around. He had his hand down there and he was pushing the poor limp thing, like a little frightened animal, towards us. I suddenly felt such pity for him that I didn't know if I'd be able to speak. Helen put her hands over her eyes and Eileen was suddenly crying. For a brief moment I thought of my mother – her neat feet moving heel and toe, heel and toe – across the kitchen floor. Then I thought – this is quite easy, I can do this.

Mr Jones, I said. The power and anger in my voice frightened me. I sounded as bad as the science teacher at school. Mr Jones, I said again, in that strange booming voice.

I imagined myself stuck there forever, saying his name again and again. I'd forgotten what else I was meant to say. My heart was pulsing in my ears, my head felt horribly swollen. Three Garibaldi biscuits were still neatly arranged on their paper doily. Mum, Mum, please don't dance. It's silly. Eileen was moving towards the door. What a coward. As I watched her, the words I rehearsed came back.

Mr Jones. You must put that thing away. You must stop doing that at once. You are letting yourself down and everyone else as well.

Nothing happened. My hands were sticky from the lemon squash. I couldn't look at Helen or Eileen. The budgerigars in their cages were purring and burbling. The kitchen felt like a cage. The three of us were budgerigars, trapped there forever, our heads nodding endlessly back and forth.

Do you hear what I'm saying? I said. You do understand?

Although I had imagined this scene many times, my fantasies had only ever stretched as far as the words I would say. I had never considered what might, or might not, happen afterwards. So it came as a surprise to me when Mr Jones cleared his throat, smiled slightly, shrugged and then hurriedly did up his trousers.

Right, I said. Eileen and Helen, please help to clear away. I knew somehow that this was important. We couldn't just leave. We had to make it all seem pleasant and normal. Helen put the squash away in the cupboard and I finished washing up the glasses. I asked Mr Jones if Ida would be going to another show soon. Mr Jones said that she would, as he put the Garibaldis in a tin.

Thank you, I said. Thanks very much, Mr Jones. We did enjoy seeing the budgerigars. Helen and Eileen mumbled thanks as well and we all walked out of the door, trying to look as normal as possible. I put my chin up high to show I didn't care. Blood was still burning in my cheeks. The street appeared to have shrunk, everything in it looked ridiculously small and fragile. It was all just so many children's toys.

In silence we walked up towards the sluice gates but as soon as we were on the flatter ground Eileen turned on me. How could you? You stupid fool? What do you think you sounded like? Then she started to cry again and ran away down the bank.

She's in love with him, Helen said.

Don't be so stupid.

No. She is. But what you did was right.

Back then, we never touched. No one did. But now Helen reached out her hand towards me. We both laughed nervously. Suddenly I felt as tall as the sky, as the tower of the Stump, and big enough to step right across the wide river. I know Helen felt it too. We caught hold of each other's hands, spun round and round, laughed with our heads back, then collapsed in the grass on the riverbank, giggling and squealing, wriggling our legs. The sky was whirling around, the leaves of the trees spinning. As we lay in the grass, Helen's head was close to mine and we looked at each other deeply for a long time, smiled, laughed again.

After that Eileen never went in to see the budgerigars again but Helen and I went. We never had another problem. I told my mother what I'd done. I told you so, she said. There's no other way. You've got to take a firm line.

Not long after that, everything changed. It wasn't anything to do with Mr Jones, it was just the sixth form really. You couldn't just mess around throwing your hat in the school corridor and swapping sweets any more. We lost interest in the budgerigars. They seemed a bit childish and anyway there was too much work to do.

At Christmas Eileen left the High School because she was never going to pass any exams even though she was easily clever enough. Instead she got a job in Oldrids and started going out with Kevin Dean. One night coming back late from hockey practice, I saw her standing at the bus stop with her hair dyed blonde and smoking a cigarette.

No sooner had Eileen gone than Helen went as well because her dad got a job managing the pie factory in Grimsby. I missed her badly and walked to school alone. Once or twice during that time I went along to see Mr Jones. In the spring I helped him plant out some seedlings and he showed me how to use the long-handled secateurs to keep the edges neat. Ida won a prize in a show in Norwich. The leg fell off the spinning fairy and Mr Jones said it would be too expensive to replace.

Then I got a place in the Junior County Hockey. That was a shock. Mr Jones said – Jolly good for you – and so did my mum. I'd always loved hockey and been good at it but I'd never thought I was as good as that. Soon I had to go to practice every night. The coach said I'd make a good PE teacher and immediately I thought – yes, that's right, that's what I'll do.

Not many got a place at PE College but I did. Helen rang to tell me she had a place at Nottingham University. I was so proud of her. I didn't see Eileen but I heard she got married to a man out on the marshes. People used to see her at the market, selling fruit and vegetables. I think she also travelled around to people's houses, doing hairdressing. After that I didn't see Mr Jones much and I didn't really think of him either. Time was tumbling on, lives spreading further and faster. That world was gone.

# For You, Hannah

Oh my green-eyed gambler, you make it so very easy.

I see her standing at the side of the road, hitching a lift in the thin summer rain. She wears a short denim skirt, and strands of her pale red hair are caught in the breeze. I brake and look back. She stands near a deserted bus stop. It's the fragility of her waving arm – that's the detail that spins in my head. I put the car into reverse but then change my mind.

I am already past her, I mustn't go back. Forward, the future. I press the gear stick into first but then I see her in the side mirror, walking towards my car. Her face appears at the window. 'Shrewsbury? Are you going to Shrewsbury?' Her green eyes open wide with the question and a Welsh accent echoes in her words. Her face is long and white, her teeth uneven. She has the same pale hair.

'Yes, I am going to Shrewsbury.'

Her face opens into an easy smile. Her bag swings on her shoulder as she pulls open the car door. For a moment anger grips at my throat, and I want to shout at her to stop, but she's already sitting next to me.

I put my foot on the accelerator and the steering wheel slips in my sweating hands. As she leans down to put her bag on the floor, that thin hair falls forward revealing two sharp bones at the top of her spine. Through her damp shirt I can see her bra, embroidered with blue flowers.

I reach out and click the locks closed. Occasionally she glances sideways, expecting me to speak perhaps? The wipers creak across the windscreen. She stifles a yawn. Her nails are bitten and painted with chipped silver varnish. Who is she? A college student on her way home? Seventeen, or eighteen? Around her wrist she's got one of those leather thongs they all wear. It's threaded with green glass beads.

I reach a junction and Shrewsbury is signposted right. I turn left but she doesn't even notice because she's rifling through her bag. I glimpse a notebook, a black leather purse, a cigarette lighter. She pulls out a clip decorated with a purple flower and pulls her damp hair back into a ponytail. She smells of rain and something sweet – rose-scented soap or hand cream.

For a moment I wonder what she thinks of me. Some middle-aged bloke with a beer belly and greying hair? But, of course, she hasn't given me a thought. We reach another junction. Shrewsbury is signposted right. I turn left. She looks across at me and swallows. 'I don't think this is the right way.'

'It'll get us there.'

I need somewhere quieter, and a wall to park against. Isn't that how this is done? But I don't know this area so I just wait until I reach a narrow lane, and then turn down it. She swallows again and her hand grips at her skirt. Her eyes move down to the handle of the door. But still she doesn't believe that this can happen.

I reach a T-junction and turn right, taking care not to let the car slow.

'No, this isn't the road.' Her voice squeaks and her eyes plead. Her knees are pressed together, her face is white. The land we're driving through is flat and featureless – no convenient wood, or riverbank, or stone wall. I swing the car left into an unmarked road. Rain is beating down on the windscreen. Her fingers scrabble on the door handle beside her. Her wrists thump at the window, the green beads slap against the glass. Who sits up waiting for this girl far into the night? Who would open the door if a policeman called?

'No through road.'

But I take that road and we drive on.

'What are you doing?' Her breath rasps, her hand clutches at the side of her seat. Still there's no place to stop. Should I turn back towards the main road? I've no sense now of where it is. Sweat runs down my cheek. I struggle to keep my foot steady on the accelerator.

Then we round a bend and come to a deserted farmyard, with a water trough and barns. Yes, this is just the right kind of place. I turn in through the gate and pull the car in tight against a wall. She's crying in strangled gasps and her knees are pressed against the door. She's pulled her bag up from the floor and is holding it tight against her.

'Please... please... no...'

I switch off the engine and turn towards her. Her eyes are shut, her shoulders shaking. She is entirely mine. I could cut her face with a knife, rip her clothes, grip her thin throat and choke the life out of her. And by the time they find her there'll be no evidence. Not a fingerprint, or the mark of a particular blade. Not even a stain. I see the knife against her throat, the hand grappling at her thighs, the blood spreading over that white shirt.

My eyes fill with red and I hear my voice spitting hot words. 'You fool. You fool, you stupid little fool. How can you be so stupid? It's all here, it's all here for you.'

Her white hand has stopped still and is spread on the glass. The purple-flower clip has fallen from her hair and lies beside the handbrake.

'Why? Why make it so easy? Why just give it all away?' My voice gives out. My mind is unravelling. My head falls forward against my hands. I suck breath into my heaving lungs and feel sweat running down my face, the salt of it touching my lips. I hold tightly to the steering wheel.

When finally I raise my head I see again the water trough, the barns. How long have we been here – two minutes? Five? I'm soaked in sweat. My body heaves and shudders. I can't bear the sight of those shaking shoulders, that tear-twisted face. I want to touch her, to comfort her. I raise my hand but she begins to scream.

'No,' I say. 'No, don't. It's all right. I'm sorry. It's just... Please...'

I want to explain but I can't find the words. I pull at the handle which winds down the window and taste the scent of wet grass and cow dung. The sound of birds twittering on a nearby telegraph pole seems suddenly loud.

She has stopped crying but her breath still comes in gasps. 'Cigarettes,' I say. 'Do you want a cigarette? They're in the glove box.'

She reaches forward and pulls out the packet and a lighter. Her hands scramble into the box and she puts a cigarette between her lips. She clicks at the lighter but the flame goes out. Her trembling hands push at it again and again but she can't make it work. I stretch out a hand and she gives me the lighter, taking care not to let our hands touch. Her head is pulled back against the seat as I click the lighter. She coughs and draws in a sobbing breath.

'I'm sorry,' I say. 'I'm sorry. But please, promise me. Don't ever do this again. Do you hear me? Don't ever, ever...'

'Take me home,' she says. 'Please take me home.'

I turn the car and pull out of the yard. She sits beside me, shivering and drawing on her cigarette. Until finally she wipes her eyes, pulls a cardigan out of her bag and wraps herself in it. The rain has stopped and a pale sun shines through a crack in the clouds. Fields fade away and are replaced by roundabouts and out-of-town supermarkets, then terraced houses and parked cars. Somehow we have reached Shrewsbury.

'Let me out here,' she says. 'Now.'

'No, I'm going to take you to where you live.'

She doesn't want that but I insist.

When I stop at the end of her road, she scrambles out of the car, holding her bag against her. 'You bastard.' Then she shouts it. 'Bastard.' She wants to stride away with head held high but her steps are unsteady, as though walking must be re-learnt.

She's forgotten to take the hair clip with the purple flower. It lies near to the handbrake and I know that later I'll pick it up and wrap my fingers tight around it. I look up and see her on the other side of the road. For a moment she stops and turns back. I raise my hand in a gesture of farewell. She begins to move that fragile arm but then changes her mind. She walks three steps, then hesitates again. I see her suck at the breeze as it blows on her face. Yes, breathe it all in, my green-eyed gambler. Look at the evening sun glistening on the puddles, the plane trees, the parked cars. Look – because you can.

# The Last House on the Marsh

Here there is no divide between land and sea, just a blur of blue where the mud flats rise. Then miles of waterlogged green, heavy with the smell of salt and rot, running right up to the sea wall which zigzags all across this land, holding back the treacherous waters of the Wash. This is a land borrowed from the sea, a land so flat it ends only where the curve of the earth falls.

Across this land a motorbike stutters, suddenly roars. Turning off the main Boston Road, it cuts along lanes edged by dykes. Cows raise their heads, butterflies shimmer along low hedges. A scatter of startled birds blooms from a twisted tree. The warm salt wind ruffles the marsh grasses and the fields of billowing corn. Still the motorbike comes. It turns right in Burton Feldyke, onto Skidds Lane, past the village hall and the red-brick bungalows.

Nellie Lancing is cutting her lawn with shears. The lawn mower broke a year ago. She hears that distant motorbike whine. A birdwatcher, or some young chap from Boston who fancies a dip in the creek? Five minutes later, stopping to ease her back, she sees a figure at her gate. Lost, she thinks. She never has visitors. Only Ted from the Fruit and Veg, the vicar, or occasionally an RSPB volunteer.

Nellie doesn't usually let people through the gate. You have to be careful. You never know who might be sizing up the place. But the motorbike man is already striding up the cracked cement path, his steps both purposeful and uncertain, his waterproof jacket rustling. A white hand moves up and tugs the helmet off.

Hello. Will. William. Perhaps you don't remember. Great-nephew.

Under the waterproof, his body is narrow, his trousers belted low at the hips. He wears a tight jumper with a T-shirt underneath. A ring pierces his ear and his hair hangs to his shoulders. An expensive-looking camera is slung around his neck. As he looks into Nellie's eyes, another face swims back to her from the past. The boy presses her hand hard – but then his tapering fingers slacken and slide out of hers.

The face is newborn, unprepared, but she knows it immediately. The dead made flesh. The shears nearly drop from her hand. Why would he come? She sent him some money and a card on his eighteenth birthday but she'd never expected to see him. His face is paper pale, his eyes chestnut brown. A few pimples gather close to his nose. His lips are raw and bitten, sparse stubble covers his chin.

Nellie finds herself staring at the shears which she has put down on the garden table. Nothing has changed and yet he is here. What does he want? Nellie has nothing to give. The boy is saying something about work experience in Lincoln, physiotherapy. He failed some of his exams. Would have called first but he couldn't find the number.

Nellie, suddenly conscious of the unravelling sleeve of her jumper, motions to the bench under the apple tree and he sits down. She has only coffee to offer, no milk. He doesn't seem to want coffee. She can't take in his words but notes that studied ease, that openness of look, which come from an expensive education. Yet his hands flutter, his face is pinched.

His eyes roam round the garden, the geraniums in their terracotta pots, the wind-scoured red-brick house with its peeling window frames, the hedge she has allowed to grow tall, as it provides some protection from the wind, and much else besides. The boy's face is amused, condescending. Clearly the family home is not what he expected. He takes out a cigarette and lights it with clumsy hands.

Silence falls between them. Above them seagulls wheel and shriek. From out on the marsh, the salt wind carries the yelps of excited children inland. The tide is out so they're catching crabs or making mud slides. It's not the same as Skegness or Mablethorpe but there's still laughter to be had if you don't mind the mud. The boy's cigarette has blown out and he lights it again, drawing in deep breaths.

So how is your father? Nellie asks.

A sudden bitterness clouds the boy's eyes, he shakes his head, blows smoke from between his teeth. Oh, he's all right, the boy says. Same as ever. I haven't seen him for a while. How long since you last saw him?

Seventeen years perhaps? You must have been three then.

Oh well, I don't suppose you would find him much changed. He never changes.

So there's been a row, Nellie thinks. The seed of it was already there the last time she visited. The wavering three-year-old, standing amidst the overgrown daisies, crying at the barking dog in the lane. His father laughing, mocking, telling him to grow up. And physiotherapy in Lincoln? That can't have been part of the plan. Surely this young man was intended for London, for work as a solicitor, or something similar.

Nellie knows how such rows can be. She remembers her older brother Henry. That boorish certainty passed down in the bone marrow of the family. Tolerance, difference, all mown down in the great drive towards some supposedly better life. Tenderness, concern are such small weapons to raise against such men. Resistance ends in the bottle or the shotgun or both.

You sent that card and the money, the boy says. You said I could come.

Of course. Of course.

He asks if she has any family photographs. He's doing an evening course in documentary photography and his project is about family history. He wanted to be a photographer, he says, but he couldn't make any money doing that. Nellie thinks with shame of the holes in the carpets, the broken tread on the stair, the old sofa blocking the hall which needs to go down to the tip. When you live on your own, you let things go.

But still she picks up her cane, which is propped in the porch, and leads him into the house, up the back stairs, along the low corridor, into the back bedroom. The curtains are drawn so she pulls them open. The photographs are there on the dressing table, arranged on stained lace mats. People in fancy dress, natives of some other country you visited once but now can hardly remember. The pictures are discoloured, their moments dissolving.

My parents. Here. Your great-grandparents. My mother died when I was ten. They wrote it down as pneumonia. Then my father. Yes, he was a pilot. That's why this house is called the Pilot's House. It was his job to go out across the marsh to meet the ships and bring them in. A heart attack and then the tide came in. His body washed up the other side of the Haven, at Freiston Shore.

The floorboards creak. Nellie is conscious of the dust surrounding the lace mats.

My brothers. Look here. Henry, your grandfather. Yes, and Alfred. Died young. She keeps her voice steady, takes care not to look at the boy as he stares into that photograph. A mirror image. Does he see it?

So sad for you, he says.

I am eighty, Nellie says. What can one expect?

Alfred, he says. I didn't know until recently.

Nellie feels some liking for the boy then. He's said the name. On a shelf beside the dressing table are the wooden carvings of birds that Alfred liked to make. Also tiny boxes and baskets, stacked full of Alfred's treasures. Pieces of glass from the marsh, the skull of a bird, the cracked shell of an egg, turquoise and speckled even now. She passes one of the wooden carvings to the boy and he turns it in his hands.

Nellie opens a drawer, pulls out a sheaf of paper.

He liked to draw.

Nellie hasn't looked at the drawings in years. But she doesn't need to, they're often in her mind. Drawings of birds on the wing, twisting suddenly, dipping and turning, slicing the air. She'd never intended to show this boy so much.

Here – with his friend Westy.

Wearing cricket sweaters, their arms are looped over each other's shoulders, as was the way of young men then. Both look so blameless, so obviously doomed. Nellie wants to shout at them, to make sure that they hear her warning this time, even through the walls of so many years.

As Nellie leads him back downstairs, Will says he'll visit again. These family disagreements are so unnecessary. Sins of the fathers, all that. For a moment Nellie starts to feel some pity for him but cuts off that feeling at its root. She mutters some polite response, hopes he has understood that she doesn't want to repeat this meeting.

After he's gone, Nellie pours herself a whisky, her hand gripped on the side of the kitchen sink. She heads to the gate, walks across the field to the sea wall. For a moment she looks inland, sees the pylons, the telephone wires looping. And the tower of Boston Stump, that one vertical in so many layers of horizontals. Parents are shepherding their children in off the creek now. Their legs caked with dried mud, they trail nets and damp towels. Stopping to tip up buckets of crabs, they holler and jig with delight as the crabs run back into the creek.

The tide is coming in, the day waning. The sky is banked with pleated clouds, rolling ever onwards across the unceasing sky. In the far distance, the silver light of the sun touches on the edge of a formless cloud. Same house, same view, same tides washing in. She thinks then of Alfred, sees him far out on the marsh.

Drawing, or carving, or running after the birds, his arms flailing. A black silhouette against the mellow rays of the washed sunlight.

Alfred – his hands feathery as he played the piano. When he was younger, before all the trouble began, he used to sit in the window seat with Westy, who walked across from the village. His father was the baker there. Together they made up comic songs, Alfred playing and Westy singing. Or made daisy chains which they looped around her neck.

That was before Westy had joined the RAF, gone up to Coningsby. Alfred had taken the bus then to see him, or pedalled on his bicycle. Nellie had tried to warn him. So many times Alfred went – until Westy went out to Malaya. Or was it Kenya? He'd stayed out there, they said.

Two weeks later Will comes again. Nellie has just come back from Scandon Marsh. She works there as a volunteer, going on her bike now that the clutch on the car has gone. She's the RSPB's oldest Lincolnshire volunteer. At a supper in the White Hart in Boston they gave her a plaque. A hint that she should retire? But Nellie won't do that. People come from the towns and they don't understand the tides, the danger.

There's no need, she says to Will.

He's come in a car, bringing with him a borrowed lawn mower. He says he can also find someone to fix the car. And maybe ring on his mobile, find out about the phone line.

Always blows down, Nellie tells him. I don't need the mower. Ted will come soon. He does all that.

But still Will mows the lawn, so she makes him a cup of black coffee which he drinks, sitting on the bench under the apple tree. He asks about her voluntary work. Down at Scandon they have allowed Coastal Realignment. That means they have moved the sea wall, given up some land which was reclaimed centuries before.

Meetings had been organised in the village hall. Better for wildlife, they were told. Better to let this bit go, make the whole coast safer. Many shouted those arguments down. What we need is solid investment in coastal defences. This is the most fertile land in England. Shelves in food shops stacked high with potatoes, carrots, lettuce, beans – all brought down from Lincolnshire. All across the world the sea levels are rising.

That'll be for your generation, Nellie says to Will.

She remembers the floods of 1953. Up in the north of Lincolnshire people were swept out of their bedroom windows, such was the force. Maurice came from the village in one of the farm trucks. No time to take anything except a coat and a change of clothes. Skegness, Mablethorpe, Ingoldmells Point – all gone under. The roads submerged, the trains stopped, the telephones down. Great black sheets of water spread over the land. They gave out that three hundred died – everyone knew it was more. Most of the bodies were never recovered.

After the water retreated, Nellie came back to the Pilot's House. Everything was covered with a layer of grey slime which took days to wash out. Sheep were dead against the field gate, their coats grey and flattened, their stomachs swollen and breaking open, flies gathering. You had to keep a handkerchief pressed to your face. Even a year later the smell still clung to the earth. The cricket pavilion from the village had been washed down and sat perched across the sea wall. Nellie is glad to have seen the worst.

She does not tell Will any of that. Soon enough the conversation comes around to Alfred again. Nellie knew that it would.

Can I ask you? I loved those drawings.

Nellie wonders what he already knows.

He died in an Asylum, she says. Or he should have done. Rauceby Asylum. But he finished up at North Sea Camp. It was a Borstal then, just across the Haven. We never did know why he was taken there. It was after the war – and the floods just a few months before.

And that was where it happened?

Yes. On the marsh there. No one knew how he got the gun.
You didn't try?
No. No. What was there to know? He was gone.

That night Nellie sits at the kitchen table. Wind is worrying in
the chimney and the sky is Bible black. The roof of the shed is
rattling. She must get it nailed down sometime. But now Nellie
finds herself short of breath, her blood pumping fast. Images rise
up and take hold of her mind. Alfred sitting at the desk in the
sitting room, his head down, his ink pen digging into the paper,
writing for hours without stopping. Nellie had believed he was
writing a book. Until the day came when she looked at the page
and none of it made any sense.

Then he was dancing out on the marsh. People thought he
was trying to catch birds but Nellie knew it wasn't that. Perhaps
if he drew them often enough he would grow wings. Surely none
of it mattered? The Pilot's House is the last on the marsh. Nellie
could keep things private. Yet one is always at the mercy of the
world. And Alfred did keep going to Coningsby, even when he
knew that Westy was not there.

It was late August when they came to take him. A stifling,
stagnant day with a low mist settled on the marsh. They came
without any warning, no letter or message. A low black car
parked close to the house. Men from the Asylum and the police.
Ropes and nets as though they had come to hunt a wild animal.

Quietly, quietly he went, with no need for the ropes or nets.
Nellie asked them not to take him, she pleaded with them and
cried, tugging at the sleeve of one of the doctors. He is quite
happy, she said. He is very happy. But she was only a girl of
twenty and they were men.

The next time Will comes, he tells her he has been to the Records
Office in Lincoln. Why? Why? What is it that he wants? He
thinks all these questions will lead to healing but they will not.
He's trying to put the words together so that they make sense.

116

Nellie also had attempted that, after Alfred was gone. Hours and hours she'd spent, reading those garbled pages. But she could find no pattern, no explanation, no story to tell.

Will also needs a story. But the one he's creating isn't true. She's not a poor old lady, shut up out on the marsh all these years, grieving for the brother she lost. She may be solitary but she's always been content. She liked her old job at the Fruit and Veg, she likes her voluntary work. She has her school friend, Margery, in Spalding.

It's true that the days were cruel after Alfred went. People stared and spoke to her slowly. They thought that Alfred's problems were inherited and must soon show in her too. She did think of moving into Boston, taking a flat there. Fewer people would know her. But she couldn't sell the house. After the flood, who would want it?

Then finally an offer came which was far too low. And on the way to the solicitor's office, stopping suddenly in the street, rain beating down, the knowledge came to her that she couldn't leave. It was the skies that held her. Every day – the joy of watching that vast and ever-changing spectacle of cloud and sunlight, stretching far away on every side, infinite and generous. How could she have exchanged that for a pale unchanging slice of sky seen through the window of a terraced house?

There had been offers of marriage but she hadn't wanted that. Maurice, whose family ran the Fruit and Veg, had always been her friend. Later she'd worked for him as a farm secretary, organising the lorries and the delivery men. That was before the foreigners came. And even though Maurice is dead now, his son Ted will always come if she needs anything. They aren't family but the loyalty is the same.

She says to Will – I think it's better if you don't come again.

Autumn is coming now, the evenings are shorter, the chill of winter blowing in. The fields are ploughed and the birds are gathering on the telephone lines. Will is standing at her gate, ready to put his helmet on. He's sorry, he says. He never intended to cause any offence. She wishes him well and waves goodbye, shuts the gate, goes to find a padlock. You have to be careful.

How dare he assume she doesn't know? Later, much later, she went to the Asylum. Time had unfolded a new world then – even in Burton people smoked strange-smelling herbs, wore orange trousers and high cork-soled shoes. In the local paper it was advertised – Open Day. A spacious summer day, the sun lost behind high cloud, the wind bringing in the smell of salt. Rain had fallen the night before and turned every leaf a brilliant green.

Nellie recognised the wide corridors and high windows from her former visits but nothing more. Everywhere now was muffled by carpet, the doors closing with a pneumatic hiss, an exhibition of landscape paintings spread along the walls. The windows hung open and potted plants covered the sills. Women were unloading home-made cakes from the backs of cars. It seemed like a village fête or a holiday camp.

Nellie had never intended to ask any questions. It was a former nurse who recognised her, remembered. Mr Roberts seemed no more than a teenager but he was the Director. In his office, model trains were displayed on a shelf. The high arched window hung open, an owl made of rattan was blowing in the breeze. Outside a brass band was playing, its sound both pompous and playful.

Nellie was like an animal caught in a trap. Pulling and pulling against the metal brace but she could not get out. In the cellars they had all the files from way back. Inside Alfred's file was a sheaf of papers, cramped handwriting enclosed in black boxes. A letter she had sent to Alfred with a chain of daisies painted down the side in watercolour. Nellie tasted something unpleasant in her mouth. That cake? Curry? It couldn't be. Cakes don't have curry in them. She worried that she might be sick.

A man born into the wrong era, they said. It'd be different now.

As she was leaving, Nellie trapped her hand in the car door crushing two of her nails. Two miles down the road she stopped in a layby, gripping her crushed fingers to her chest, swallowing sobs. It was only ten miles further to North Sea Camp. As she drove through Boston and out the other side, the temperature dropped and the wind rose. A spray of rain gusted across the windscreen.

North Sea Camp – a low straggle of buildings, surrounded by wire fences, glass-topped walls and security gates. She drove on past it, on towards the sea. The marsh here is like her own marsh – but wilder, ragged, brutal. Here you feel the whole of the North Sea pressing in and hear the distant smash of waves. Nellie was wearing only a summer dress, a thin cardigan. Her sandals had open toes but still she walked out along the creeks. The fine rain was coming in like so many grey curtains closing again and again.

Was it here that Alfred died, or a little further out? She didn't know. It was hard to see. She wiped rain from her eyes. Surely there must be some trace of him. But there was only the water bubbling in the creeks, driftwood, cigarette ends, the sole of a shoe. A plastic bag, caught on a log, tugged by the wind. Then just to taunt her, or so it seemed, a bang like a gun. She braced herself then, ready to run to his side. But it was only a young man with a motorbike, that was all.

Christmas comes and Nellie wonders about Will. Should she send a card? She doesn't have the address. Ted and his family ask her over for Christmas lunch, as they always do. January edges forward, day collapsing into day, each one the same. Nellie cycles out to Scandon. The bins are overflowing with coffee cups, sandwich wrappers, nappies. She has to call the Council three times to get everything cleaned up.

A fierce storm is forecast. Nellie listens to the local news on the radio. A tidal surge. Samuel, the old chap who organises the volunteers, comes out to say that they're closing up at Scandon, putting the red flags out. They can't take the risk. But the pumping stations at Burton and Slippery Gowt have both been upgraded. They will hold.

As the day passes, the sky turns gunmetal grey and lies low and heavy over the marsh. Soon the rain comes down in torrents, smashing against the shed and the windows of the house. Nellie carries the bench in from the garden, wobbles on a ladder, wrapped in her oilskin, to whack an extra nail into the corrugated iron on the shed roof. Should she lift the carpets? They're hardly worth saving. Last time the water was a foot deep in the bedrooms. It'll not come so high this time.

On the news it says that a bus has been blown off the road at Spalding. The high tide is due at seven. See how high that comes. Then it'll all become clear. At five o'clock news comes from further up the coast, Scarborough. People are hanging onto lamp posts so they don't get blown over. No harbour wall any more, it's all gone under. Nellie pushes jumpers, trousers, underwear into a canvas holdall and waits by the door. Such is the howl of the wind, she never hears the car, only sees the headlights, and Ted hurrying up the path, head ducked down.

Nellie. Come on, love. Best get you shifted.

Ted helps her to lock the front door – as though that will keep the water out. He holds her tight as they edge down the garden path. A gust hits them and he steadies her. The garden is sodden, plants beaten flat. The back hedge is straining sideways, its branches cracking. Ted's heavy-duty lantern touches on the gate, the car ahead, a tide of water flowing down the lane.

We need to keep hold of the car door, he says. Come on, Nellie, hold on here.

The door is nearly ripped from his hands. Nellie reaches out and together they hold it. Get in, get in. Nellie pulls herself into the car and Ted slams the door. Soon he appears on the other side, stooped and battered, pulling his door open, keeping it gripped tightly as he edges into his seat. As Ted starts the car and turns, the headlights move along the sea wall, such a small and fragile bank.

What are they saying? Nellie asks.

Bad, Ted says. Worst in sixty years. Let's hope they're wrong. I think you'll not stay in the village. Spalding may be best.

Margery will take me.

Yes. Maybe John with the tractor.

They can't see more than a few feet ahead. A crack of lightning forks across the sky, revealing for a moment a stunned landscape. The car headlights illuminate a shimmering wall of rain. The windscreen wipers screech backwards and forwards. The water is lying an inch thick on the road. Ted raises his foot slowly from the clutch, keeps the engine revving fast. A rotary clothes drier blows across, scratching against the car. Nellie raises her hands, frightened that the windscreen may break. Even though Ted knows the road, he nearly drives into the dyke at the end of Skidds Lane. As he edges the car back, Ted and Nellie give way to choked laughter.

Did they get the sheep in?

Oh yes. Yes.


At the edge of the village men are out in fluorescent jackets. Ted opens the car window. A dustbin lid dances across the road. The policeman ducks and shouts a warning. Nellie stares across to where the lights of Boston should be but sees nothing. The policeman says – Anyone else to come?

Only Samuel now.

Outside the village hall, the vicar takes hold of Nellie's bag, offers his arm.

Ah, good to see you, Mrs Lancing. Best not to risk it.

A slap of wind buffets against her, blowing her breath back down her throat. Wellingtons splash through waves of gathering water. Lights shine out, blurred, from the village hall. A father carries two sleeping infants, wrapped in blankets, their heads resting on his shoulders. Lanterns dance across the car park and distant roofs, sparkle on the black slick of surface water.

Don't let them get settled, a policeman says. The vans are coming.

Nellie has done this before. It's difficult for the younger people, those with families. They don't know. Nellie helps the vicar's wife lay out mugs on a tray, finds milk and biscuits. The biscuits look stale but never mind. Children are playing hopscotch, and swinging from the wall bars, at the end of the hall.

Nellie, there's a young man, the vicar says.

Oh. No. Him?

Nellie turns back to the urn. The water gushes out, scalds her hands. Nellie jiggles the lever, burning her fingers, but it won't turn off. Boiling water is spraying all around, steam is filling the kitchen. The vicar's wife wraps Nellie's hand in a tea towel, gets hold of the lever, twists it off.

For pity's sake, she says. Like we need more water.

Hysterical laughter cackles all about.

Nellie dabs at her hand.

Is it burnt? Are you all right?

Oh no, no. No problem at all.

But Nellie's hand rages and throbs. Not as bad as the car door but bad enough. Some of the biscuits are soaked now, as well as being stale. Outside a siren is blaring. A policeman enters the hall. OK. OK. Listen now. Everyone will be moving on soon. No need to panic. Yes, the sea defences are down in Mablethorpe but they always have it worse than us. No, best to avoid Boston. If you do have friends or relatives we'll do our best to get you there. Nellie slips past him and pushes her way into the loos.

She reaches for the switch but no light comes on. She flicks it a few times. Must be the fuse, maybe the water has got in. Above her, furred light seeps through frosted glass. Police radios are crackling, gabbling words from other planets. Despite her jumper and waterproof, Nellie is shaking.

She rests her hands against the cracked tiles next to the basins and waits. Her face looms at her from the mirror, like something rising up from underwater, staring, soaked and shocked. A sob rises and she wipes her hand across her mouth. What am I doing? Shut in the loos of the village hall, terrified of a boy and the damage his kindness might do.

Did he really come on his motorbike all the way from Lincoln? Just to look for her? He must be mad. She hears Ted's voice. Come along now. The vans are here. A child is keening. A clamour of voices suddenly rises. The cellars of the Stump are filling. New boilers down there cost one hundred thousand pounds. The banks of the Haven cannot hold.

It took Alfred four days to die. The morning of the fourth day, that's when his soul was finally taken. He'd shot himself in the head but the bullet hadn't gone right through. You'd have thought he could at least have fired straight. Nellie had managed to get into Boston then, flagged down a stranger on a motorbike. Her skirts pulled up to her waist, her chest pressed against the man's leather jacket, hair blown in her mouth.

When they changed the dressings she saw the blood matted in Alfred's hair, the blackened flesh where his cheek had been, a piece of bone, bright white, splintered. But he wouldn't die, he wouldn't. So that fourth morning, the last, she'd gone outside into the Bath Gardens, sat under a cedar tree. The first ray of sun in a long while. She couldn't go back, she couldn't. Only when he was dead. She'd hated him then. Others found ways of living with that stain. He had lost Westy but such things happen to many people. Why had he expected tolerance when there was none?

She became the loyal and courageous sister who nursed her brother to the end.

Are all stories lies?


Nellie, Nellie, are you done, love? Still room for one more in the van. She stumbles out into the lobby. A young policeman is wiping water from his face. Rain or tears? Out on the road, everything is alight with a shower of sparks which flit across the water, fizzle and bang.

Shorted out the mains. Never mind, plenty of powerful lanterns.

From the dark hall, she hears Will's voice – high pitched and weeping.

No, she says to the policeman. No. You take the van.

Nellie steps out into the shadowed hall. The vicar's wife comes forward and then retreats. The families have all gone. Only a few men stand around, mopping up or drinking tea. Nellie finds Will crouched on a low bench – the kind that children use for gym classes. He fires words at her but she can't understand them.

The men in the hall and the vicar's wife are looking away, making themselves busy, washing up or switching the electrics off. Nellie feels the boy's burning rage, his raw hurt. Will he not learn? We'd all like to grow wings and fly away. She sinks down beside him on the bench, stretches out her hand.

Samuel stamps into the hall, followed by two policemen. Voices are joining together in tortured chorus. The sea defences are down in Boston. Crashed right over the bank. Like bloody Venice. Tower Street, Church Street, Wormgate – and still rising. Soon be up to the top of the bridge. Sea wall at Slippery Gowt. No, no. Yes. Gone as well. God help us. What will be spared now? Who?

# Smooth and Sleek

how can I tell you it is like this in the town we have been waiting
we wait and wait from the radio we hear the news most have left
but it is not certain some people say stay some say go mostly they
say to the young people like me you must go and hide yourself

I have always wanted one. I remember when I was a kid – there
with my dad in the hot tarmac car park at the pub. An Aston
Martin Lagonda parked right there. Of course, I didn't know
the name or the make then. Also it's fair to say that even then
there was criticism of that car. Some of the mechanics were
totally unreliable. And that paper dart look? Well, it's a matter
of opinion. But I just knew. Standing there with my bottle of
Coke, greedy kid's eyes running along the line of the bonnet.
Edging my shoulder secretly along the paintwork just for the
ecstasy of it.

of course there is no food all phone lines are dead but just once
twice someone gets a call maybe it is better here or there I do not
think so I decide to stay this is a small town maybe the soldiers
will just pass through and go on to the coast also this is not a bad
place to hide many caves and also houses burnt out with deep
cellars no one cares about people such as me which now maybe
is good

*

Yes, that car. Perhaps in reality most of the choices I have made were about the car. Not directly perhaps but still. Even at that age, I knew that car cost forty thousand pounds so you're never going to own a car like that if you don't make money. So I went into finance. It was a natural choice for me because I was good at maths and find it easy to talk to people. But all the time I was thinking – directly or not – that as long as I kept getting promoted, one day I would do it. I'd walk into the showroom and spend the money. I'd buy myself an Aston Martin.

we listen to the shelling and it comes closer a group of us stay in the remains of a house near the outskirts of the town this house still has electricity although why we do not know for weeks now no electricity and not much water you must walk to an old well was closed off many years ago but dug open now

Of course, I did think about going second hand. That was in my early twenties. I remember going over those ads until the paper had worn thin, pricing it all up but, in all honesty, I didn't feel confident – even though there was so much less choice at that time. Maybe at some deeper level, I just wasn't ready.

remember the day when they come we knew well the cellar was ready with tins and buckets we think maybe we will be safe this cellar has another door a place where coal was get in so you may still get out through this other door if the need is happen we will go out of that door by order of age youngest to go first I am the fourth youngest

Other people were putting down deposits on flats – but who wants a flat when you can have an Aston Martin? Really I am just not a man for second hand. It's a bit like the first relationship. It's got to be special, perfect. But every week I looked at the ads. You know, with Aston Martins, it's that marriage of power, beauty and soul. The perfect proportions, flowing bodywork, cosseting interiors.

they will not find this place easy we look at the ceiling carefully this place will not come down except a direct hit we are there four days hear the breath that draw before a bomb falls shells fall the whole earth shake voices we do not understand eat fish and tomatoes from tins and drink little water some hours of peace they have taken all and move on now

Sorry. I am doing my best to tell you this but there is quite a bit of background noise. So anyway, my thirty-fifth birthday and I'd already got the mortgage on the flat and the right relationship. So then I thought – yes, now. But still it was a hard decision. Aston Martin make quite a few different models and there is a lot of debate. It depends what you want to do with it, of course. But you get on these internet forums and one person tells you this car has better handling, this is a better transmission system, the trim on this one is not the best quality.

please I am asking would you listen carefully I know it is difficult with this disturbance so we think it is best we do not move for we have tins and water enough wait wait wait the air is close and only two or three chinks of light people just lying on the floor not talking until an evening comes when we hear voices then banging on a door that leads in the back of this house know we are trapped with our eyes we ask each other is it time now to run out still we wait

Sorry. Is that better now? Can you hear? Anyway, where was I? Yes, if I'm honest, part of the pleasure was the choosing. You ask yourself questions about the lifestyle you've got. For example, are you really going to get much use out of a convertible? And speed – well, all the Aston Martins have speed, of course, but how much do you really need?

*

hope that you can hear me I am trying hard to be clear my story
I hope will be received with respect so comes that day we know
that all is ended someone pushes the person who is first and that
one goes the door breaks down a great shouting and terror starts
it is known what these soldiers do someone grabs me and pushing
me out of the hole into the glaring light of the street

Sorry for this noise. Can you hear me now clearly? Good. Then
after that there's the showroom. Of course, you can just wander
in and take a look but it's best to book an appointment. It doesn't
matter how many times you do that. From their point of view,
they want you to take time to decide because it's a disaster if you
finish up less than satisfied.

it is difficult for me to speak but I must we are not listened to
again and again we try to speak but no one will listen so I will
go on after the cellar I come up into the town and run all is
smoking rubble the air full of dirt two bodies dead on the steps of
a church a voice on a microphone is shouting I run across where
a square used to be this a small town you only pass a few streets
and you are in the hills I run dancing from one corner to the next
so I go on think that soon I will be away but then just as I run
out round a corner I go direct into him he points a gun at me his
beard is matted his clothes black with oil one of his front teeth
knocked in he shouts at me words I do not understand

Yeah, OK, we'll just have to do our best to ignore the noise. The
next bit I want to say is – you can also test drive, of course. And
that is awesome, believe me, awesome. Because those cars – when
you slide into the seat, it is as though the car has suddenly been
built around you. It fits you exactly, like a bespoke suit. Then
there's the finish. Now that itself takes a bit of thought. Me, I
finally settle on Concours Blue. Subtle, understated but elegant.
For the interior, I settle on the Caithness leather in cream truffle.

*

the time has come for me to speak no matter what now I must speak in this situation I have already smeared my face thick with dirt and put on clothes like an old man this everyone must do you hide whether you are man or woman you try to make yourself a part of the rubble only but still I see the light in this mans eye I know what must come but I make signals to him I am putting my hands to my mouth as though to say you are hungry if I can give him food then maybe just two streets from here is the house once lived in by my aunt she buried food there

Oh for God's sake. This is beginning to annoy me. You just want to speak about something and you find you can't get a word in edgeways. Anyway, the point is, when you drive – the car just slides away from you. It feels as smooth as the flow of a river. Every detail is perfect. That passion, that craftsmanship, that determination not to compromise. That specific combination of refinement, luxury and genuine materials. It makes you feel how extraordinary it is to live in the modern age. A world where engineering can be developed to this pinnacle, where man can make something so sublime.

please please will you just let me speak I beg you please so this man I beckon to him now the streets here are empty so we walk and the pavement is some place melted under our feet he comes up beside me puts out his hand to touch my cheek I smile at him rather sweetly though I am choking with fear at my aunts house there is still the kitchen just as before the war most has been taken but the table is still there he follows me as I go in the back kitchen which is built in the hill I do not want him with me in that tight space I have to bite hard to stop myself screaming I pull the wooden cabinet out of the way and dig out the floor tiles here is the hidden box where she puts the tins

God, you would think if you asked someone to be quiet then

they would do it, wouldn't you? I've got as much right to talk as anyone else. So anyway, well, it doesn't all go entirely smoothly because once I've finally made my order and the guy has checked all the details. All that is done and two weeks have passed. So I know it's stupid of me but I just realise that the cream truffle leather isn't a good idea. I get in touch with some people online and they confirm what I know in my heart – which is that cream leather is going to look great for a year. Maybe two years or even three. But finally it isn't going to wear well. So that will affect the resale value of the car. Now I'm not thinking of selling. This is a purchase for the long term. But still. The problem is – have I left it too late to change?

I will go on I and people like me we have been silenced long enough I get out tinned pork and potatoes beans and cooking fat also a bottle of wine I take them in the kitchen as I pass the window I see briefly the bright orange of the sun setting even through the smoke so he and I sit down and he opens the tins with the point of a knife we eat then together straight from the tins he pushes the pork and the beans down in the cooking fat and eat how can I eat when I know what is going to happen only because I am so hungry who knows when or if I will eat again with his dirty finger he pushes in the cork of the bottle after he drinks he smiles at me and stretches out his hand again to touch my cheek he says to me girlfriend and then he gives me drink and I pour down much for to make my mind blind it will not help to fight this I have been told by others so I smile at him sweetly I take his hand he pushes his thick and dirty fingers down then between my legs and laughs and I try to laugh as well at least I am twenty-six years old I have known a man before it is worse for those that have not

Shut up, would you? Shut up? Anyway, I rang the dealership and I was pretty worried. But you know what? The guy I spoke to was really great, so polite and helpful. He said he'd ring through to the workshop. After only ten minutes he rang back and said I could make a change. Now that, you see, is a really excellent level of service. He said to me – Sir, it is vitally important to us that this car is exactly what you want. People can say – oh it's just too much money. But you see why you are paying that kind of money. This is an individual service. It is about people who really care.

no I will not be quiet I have been silenced long enough for years now we ask the international community please help us but no no no so I undo my shirt for him smile smile it matters only that you stay alive we have shared a meal together surely I will be saved I pull down my trousers and he pads his hands all across me grunting and grabbing I can do this it is not too much problem but soon he pushes me around the other way then I plead with him please the cooking fat he sees and pushes his hand into the pot smears the fat on that part of me I am glad of this for the pain is less

I have a right to tell my story too. You people. It's always about you and your problems, isn't it? So anyway. I am just going to continue. So this is it – then comes the day when you go to collect what you've ordered. In my case, I finally decided on a Rapide S. Now there is much debate about this particular model. Inevitably some people don't rate it. They say that the steering is too heavy, that the new eight-speed gear box doesn't really improve shift quality, that the low driving position means limited visibility. But finally you have to know what feels right for you. There's always going to be someone telling you that you've made the wrong decision.

listen please listen I need someone to listen to hear this is my life this is what happened to me he and I are in that house together four days we eat he sleeps on the sofa when he wakes he calls me and makes me sit on him rubbing his dirty hands inside me or pushes me over the back of the sofa do it like that I find a guitar that is still there in my aunts cupboard and I play for him this makes him smile and say again and again girlfriend girlfriend once afterwards he does me then starts to cry and cries many tears shows me photographs of his home and his family when he sleeps I think that I should try to run but where would I go is there anywhere safer here we have food I do not think he will kill me I have been good to him

I'm not listening. No, I am not. I have listened enough. Why should I always be made to feel guilty about this stuff? So anyway – believe me, when I got there, to pick up the car. It is the end of a long process, there are so many choices to be made, so many things they check. You can only admire that attention to detail. And when you see your car there, you know that it was all worth it. All the work, all the decisions, all the discussions you've had with people. Then when you drive it away. I mean, for me, it was an early summer day and I wound down the window and just drove through the countryside for an hour or more. I won't deny it. I was close to tears.

and this then is what I want you to understand if you come to our God forgotten country and look in through the smashed windows of that house and you see us sit together you think how good and pleasant is this a man and his girlfriend are enjoying a meal together this is what you see and this is what you think and this is what I cannot I cannot

OK. That really is enough now. You got the message at last, did you? I mean, I've really been perfectly polite. Of course, I'm sure you think – well, it's just a car. But it isn't actually. That's the point. It's important to me. And I've got as much right to tell my story as anyone else. So there's no need for you to look at me like that.

# The Stop

James and I are arguing as we often do – without enthusiasm, our words spiteful but slow. He's accusing me of failing to take any interest in his work. I'm suggesting, gently, that perhaps he's having an affair with one of his female colleagues, even though I know that that isn't true. Long silences emerge between our barbed words. I look across at James and wonder – as I have wondered for the last twenty years – how much longer will this last?

It's a late summer evening and we're driving back from a weekend away. I smoke a cigarette, knocking ash out of the open car window. We pass through a small town called Ledbury then find that the road ahead is blocked. James takes a side road and we find ourselves rolling down lanes which twist and turn, rise and fall, grow narrower and narrower. Trees grow thickly overhead, shutting out the light. How much longer?

Our car dips through the underwater light, making no more sound than a breath of wind. Sometimes a shaft of sunlight pierces the shadows. The steering wheel threads through James's hands. We cross a narrow bridge, and pass a postbox in a red-brick wall. The day has been warm, and now, after a sudden splatter of rain, a thin vapour rises from the ground. The car tyres brush against wet grass. Through the open car window there's a smell of decay, the first sign of autumn. We round a bend, and come face to face with the falling sun. Both of us blink as rainwater on the windscreen shatters in the sudden light.

And it's then that the woman rushes into the road. Grey hair blown like thistledown, red socks under a tweed skirt. Her thick hand dashes through the air. James brakes hard, and I am flung forward against the seat belt. My head jerks towards the windscreen then thuds back against the seat. The car comes to a stop inches from the woman. She thrusts her hand at us again then she draws back, peering at us through stunned eyes, and comes to the window. I hear her breath snagging in her throat. Her lips are folded in, and her pale eyes water.

'Please,' she says. 'Please. My friend. She's fallen...'

James pulls the car onto the verge. In the hedge two yew trees form an overgrown arch which rises above an open wooden gate. James and I get out of the car. Wet grass clings to my bare legs and the hem of my skirt. Below us a low white cottage is settled at the bottom of a bank. It has a sagging roof and metal window frames. Rows of vegetables and flowers grow up to the front windows.

The woman stumbles down the path, her hands gathering her apron into a ball. The door is open, and she disappears inside. The hall is low and cramped with steep stairs, and a carpet worn to string. The wallpaper is brown with a faded pattern of bamboo. There's a smell of rainwater and sap. James's foot catches against wellington boots lined up on the quarry-tiled floor. They topple sideways, one against another, in a domino fall.

Through a door to the left, in a narrow sitting room, the woman squeezes her weight between a sofa and an armchair. A square of sun slants in through the low front window. One wall is filled by a crooked glass cabinet stacked full of dusty glasses, as delicate as spider's webs. A shelf above the gas fire is decorated with a row of china dogs. Uneven floorboards creak under our feet.

Then, over the back of the sofa, I see a woman lying on the rug. She rests on her side, one leg folded down across the other,

her hand raised as though to shield her face. Her glasses – with pink transparent frames – have fallen from her face and are open on the carpet beside her.

'Just now. She fell just now. We must get her up.' The apron woman looks to James, not me. He hesitates, then kneels beside her and takes hold of her wrist. I feel sure that he has no idea how to take someone's pulse but he plays his role with conviction, searching for a throbbing vein, peering at the face of his watch. 'We need to ring for an ambulance,' he says and goes back into the hall.

The apron woman pulls at the collar of her shirt.

'I'm sure they'll send someone straightaway.' My voice creaks in the silence. A wooden clock on the mantelpiece ticks, its face decorated with clouds and cherubs. I walk around the sofa and force myself down beside the fallen woman. One of her feet is oddly twisted. Her brown lace-up shoes are worn down on one side. They are the same shoes as the apron woman wears. A bulge of white flesh and a yellowed vest show between her skirt and jumper. A safety pin holds the waistband of the skirt.

'We must get her up,' the apron woman says. 'We must get her onto the sofa.'

I hear James's voice from the hall; he comes into the room and asks the address. For a moment the apron woman seems not to know, then the words stumble out. Still I kneel. Memory opens, and I see the life-sized doll they had in First Aid at school. Giggling, we practised mouth to mouth resuscitation on the rubber-tasting lips. But I know I shouldn't touch this woman or move her hand from her face.

'She was only...' The apron woman waves in the direction of the window. 'The garden. She was just going out into the garden.'

A dog appears, an Alsatian, slow and dusty. Its spine snakes as it walks, and its hip bones stand up high. It comes to the stricken woman, sniffs at her, and gives one brief whine. It looks up at the apron woman with tired eyes, and then it settles itself down, its nose close to the soles of the sick woman's shoes. James comes back, ducking under the low door. In this room he's too emphatic, as though a black line has been drawn around him. He keeps jostling his hands, clasping them, laying them aside, picking them up again.

'An ambulance is coming.' His voice is too loud, too insistent.

'Blankets,' the woman says.

'Yes.' Both James and I say it at once.

James comes around the sofa and kneels beside the woman, his long legs crumpled against the brick hearth. There's too little room here, between the sofa and the fireplace. The glass cabinet, the faded wallpaper, the armchair press in on us. At the window a lupin waves and dances, caught in a sudden gust of wind. Behind it the falling sun spreads a sheen across the sky, turning it pale blue and pink, like the inside of an oyster shell.

James moves the sick woman's hand from her face, holds it for a moment, uncertain, then lays it on her chest. The dog licks its lips, sniffs. The woman's body turns slightly, a twitch passes up her leg. Her face is turned to us, dimpled and powdered like the crust on bread. Beside one of her eyes there's a crack of yellow where a tear has dried. Her face shivers, she snatches a shallow gulp of air, then breathes out, long and slow. As I watch her, something changes. It's as though an invisible veil is lifted from her. Her arm slides to the floor. Perhaps this is death, I think, and am shocked at my detachment. No, no. I must be mistaken. Still the dog watches, licks its lips, yawns.

The apron woman comes back with an eiderdown, and a grey blanket with red stitching round the sides. I watch her face, waiting to see whether she registers that something has changed but she's busy with the blanket and eiderdown. She passes them over the back of the sofa and we take them and begin to lay them over the sick woman. A patch has been sewn over a hole in the eiderdown but still feathers are coming out. We pull the blanket back and forth between us, too far to one side, then too far to the other, and back again.

'How long did they say?' the apron woman asks.

James is still holding the blanket by its red-stitched edge. 'They didn't say.'

The apron woman stands quite still, staring at her friend, at the place where the invisible veil used to be. She turns to us, her gaze as scattered as sunlight. Her hands are held out in front of her as though some unseen object has just been lifted from them. Her eyes move stiffly, taking in the darkening room, the clock, the photos on the mantelpiece, the china dogs. She looks up at the ceiling and shakes her head. The corner of her mouth twists. Her hand comes up to her face, her palm locks under her jawbone, gripping her cheek. 'We've lived here forty years,' she says.

I stand up to go to her but she's brittle and steps away from me.

'Tea?' she says.

'No, you sit down.'

But she will not do that. Instead she goes out through the door at the end of the room. I follow her down two steps into a lean-to kitchen. She's pulling down cups and saucers from a yellow-painted shelf. Long-stemmed flowers are laid on the table, with newspaper underneath them, beside them a cut-glass vase and a pair of secateurs. Raindrops glisten on half-open buds. The stems of the flowers bleed onto the newspaper. The air is filled with bruised evening shadow.

I look for a kettle but there isn't one. A blackened pan stands on two electric rings and I fill it at the Belfast sink. It's absurd, of course, this tea-making pantomime but some ritual must be performed, a period of time must be filled. A saucer falls and rattles round and round on its rim but doesn't break. For a moment I wonder if I might start screaming. The woman scolds herself as milk splashes onto the sleeve of her shirt. We need to move the flowers from the table so that we can put the tray there, but instead I hold the tray while she loads the cups, teapot and milk. We go back to the sitting room. James steers the woman to an armchair, and when I give her a cup of tea, she takes it in both hands.

'Thank you,' she says. 'Thank you so much.'

I pour tea for James and pass it to him over the body of the dead woman – for surely she is dead? And so much in the way, so inconveniently situated. Shocked, I push that thought from my mind. Of course, she can't be dead. She can't really. The clock strikes and we listen as each stroke dissolves into the room. Eight o'clock. The dog stirs, raises its head from its paws, then settles again. From under the grey blanket, the dead woman's twisted foot sticks out, one lace trailing.

'Can I ring anyone for you?' James says.

The apron woman looks beyond him, lost. Then her eyes come back to him, open wide. 'Mr Webb,' she says. 'Our neighbour. At the farm. Left out of the gate.' She points her finger wildly, and shapes her mouth around the words, as though communicating with the deaf.

James lays a hand on my shoulder as he passes. I look up at him and realise how grateful I am that he is here. Then there are voices outside, blunt in the muffled air. From the window I see a man in a uniform on the path talking to James. Two more men appear at the gate. Dimmed voices and boots scuffle in the hall. The woman pulls the dog away and stands holding it by the collar. The ambulance men flick a switch, and the apron woman and I blink at each other in the naked light. The sofa is pulled back, and the armchair. The tray topples on the bureau so I seize it and hold it clamped against me. Again, I feel the instinct to scream and keep on screaming. The grey blankets and eiderdown are laid aside. They open her shirt. I turn away, my skin winces at their probing hands.

I take the tray into the kitchen. Behind me their voices sound like shouting. My heart is beating in my hands. My eyes are blurred by gathering tears. When I go back, they are lifting her gently, like a sleeping child. One leg drops down awkwardly, the knee twisting sideways. They stop and gather it up. A blanket is dropped across her face. In the hall I hear them moving the stretcher, banging against the door frames as they wrestle in the narrow space. Then they are gone, out of the door.

James's cup of tea is on the hearth. Anyway, the water was never properly boiled. I move the sofa back into position, and the armchair. The rug is crumpled where she lay. I reach down and pull it straight. On the top of the bureau her leather-strapped watch continues its muffled tick. Her ring lies beside it, a plain gold band. I stand and look at the room, recording every detail, as though leaving it after many years.

When I go out the stretcher has been carried up the path and is at the yew-thatched gate. The apron woman stands watching, her hands dangling, her mouth a little open. James is coming back along the lane accompanied by an elderly man wearing a cardigan with a zip and a pattern of diamonds. He holds a straw hat in his hands. The apron woman shakes her head at him as though in wonder. James is talking to the men who carry the stretcher. Their boots are wet from the grass verge. A car comes along the lane, brakes, slows. In the front seat two heads turn, gape, then the car accelerates, and is gone.

The woman turns to us. 'Thank you,' she says. 'Thank you so much for your help.' She pulls her grey hair back from her face with a fluttering hand. The door of the ambulance closes with a tinny thump.

'Thank you,' Mr Webb says, turning to us suddenly. 'But you must go now. You must be getting on. I'll help... I see to... Everything.'

James suggests that we should leave our numbers. There's no reason for this because there will be no papers to sign, no statements to make, no questions to answer. We will not attend the funeral because we do not know these women. And yet it seems wrong to go and leave nothing at all and so James goes with Mr Webb into the cottage to note down our numbers. I stand with the woman on the side of the road. The wind picks at the side of her apron and her grey hair. The mark is still on her sleeve where she spilled the milk. Her face is in the shadows, staring and staring down the lane.

James comes back up the path with Mr Webb. The woman calls her eyes back from far away, focuses on us, and thanks us again. The dog has followed James and Mr Webb from the house, and sits in the gateway, watching. We cross the lane to our car and get into it but James doesn't start the engine. Instead we look at each other and for once his eyes hold mine. Death should change something. It should put things into perspective, it should make us grateful. We should be gripped by a sudden love of life. At the very least we should think – guiltily – thank God it wasn't me. And we do think and feel all of those things. And at least for this brief moment I'm glad of James, glad of the frail things we share.

It will not last, of course. Tomorrow everything will go on just as before. We will forget. But James lays his hand on mine and we grip each other as though we care. We look out at Mr Webb and the woman standing together at the side of the lane. He threads the brim of his hat through his hands. She cradles an invisible baby in her arms. Both are dazed and stare at the failing sky as though it is quite new to them. The car shudders to life. We drive on.

# From Far Around They Saw Us Burn

We are the children of Cavan. Do you know of that place? It is a border town, betwixt and between, a place of crossroads – and yet strangely few pass by there. The land around is low and sodden, a place of scrub and straggly pines, lanes and paths leading nowhere. The damp comes up through the soles of your boots and clots in the lungs.

The town of Cavan itself has a wide main street of many fine buildings and yet it seems the sun never shines at an angle to touch the stonework there. Walking the main street, you pass the Central Hotel, the Farnham Arms, Fegans the Draper and Sullivans the General Store. And then, of course, the Convent buildings and the orphanage.

Those buildings are there and yet they are not. For that place is never opened up, the nuns being a closed order, so though the many windows face onto the street, the glass is opaque and obscured by bars. We orphanage girls are never seen except when we go to the cathedral for mass. And should you ever have cause to knock, the nun who unlocks the door will keep to the side so that you may not see her, for that is the way of our world.

It was the Sullivan family who knew of it first. Sitting up late in the kitchen over a game of penny poker with some of their staff who lived then on the premises, as was the way at that time. And Louis Blessing was there, he that was famous for playing football, for he was gone on Cissie Reilly as worked the grocery counter.

Over the road in Fegans, the drapery store, yet others were still awake. A group of young men returned from a badminton party, lying several to a bed, laughing and joking yet. The street lights were off, the last Garda foot patrol was back at the station. The only man abroad was James Meehan, the taxi driver, who arrived at the Farnham Arms. Later he was sure of the exact time. Ten to two.

Then come two o'clock that party at Sullivans broke up. And then it was that Cissie Reilly stood up from the card table and walked over to the window, pulled back the fringed velvet curtain, looked out into the yard to see what weather they might expect the following day. For Sullivans, you see, was next door to the Convent and overlooked the orphanage.

At first Cissie thought it was a low mist she saw. Others crowded next to her to give their opinions. The night was clear, with no sight of stars but a high, ragged moon with shreds of cloud racing past it. All were agreed. It was smoke, smoke, pumping out of a vent in the orphanage wall.

In the Sacred Heart Dormitory we orphanage girls felt it first as a settling of boards, the scraping of a hinge, a sound like a yawn, a taste of ash at the back of the throat. But we were feared to get up. Many a night we had lain there needing to relieve ourselves but too frightened to go to the pot. So though we heard Mary Caffrey's footsteps go to the cubicle to get Miss O'Reilly, still we lay rigid in our beds.

The building was without light, only the moon slanting silver at the windows. Yet we heard Mary's feet go pat-pat again down the wooden stairs to the first storey, along the corridor, up another flight of stairs to the cell of Sister Felix. Then a harsh noise broke on our ears, drilling into the restless night. It was the ringing of the doorbell at the Covent, a sound we did not oft hear.

And this was a long ring, then hardly a moment of silence, then another long ring, followed by many short jabs at the bell. So that then some of the girls who were close to the windows pulled themselves up on their beds so that they might see out. *From the laundry*, they said. *That's where it's coming.*

By then some of us older girls had gone into St Clare's Dormitory across the corridor, or even downstairs to Our Lady's. You would never generally have done such a thing but by then it was not just the bell ringing. Also from outside the gate came shouting and a blunt thumping. You might have thought it was the sound of a fist slamming, or a foot kicking, and perhaps at first it was. But soon we knew that it must be an axe which was splitting the door.

Suddenly the lights came on and we all stood blinking in our white nightdresses, standing between the six rows of iron beds. There was Veronica, Bernadette and the Carroll girls. Mary and Susan McKiernan and also Mary Lowry who wore a gold cross around her neck. She had it as a prize from the Bishop for she had a calling, was soon to become a nun.

Those up at the window whispered the news back to us. They saw Sister Felix with a key which she gave to Mary Caffrey. Surely it was the door to the main entrance of the Convent? Then another noise – raucous and jaunty. A car horn – bleeping in short bursts again and again.

Later it was recorded that it was Cissie Reilly as started the banging. For how else could they wake the sleeping nuns and alert them to the danger? Then the man from Sullivans, John McNally, was kicking with stout boots. Until those young men from Fegans drapery came, them who had returned from the badminton, who brought an axe to smash it in. Some said it was five minutes they were there, others more like ten. But they could not get in.

Louis Blessing, the football player, he had run up the road to the Garda station to raise the alarm there. As he came running back, he found James Meehan, the taxi driver, who had been sleeping with his head on the car wheel. Louis shouted at him – *Drive down the car, drive it down.* So Louis got into the passenger seat and they drove down together. Louis said – *Blast the horn, blast it loud.* But James, still half asleep, did not take his meaning so Louis leaned across and pressed on the horn again and again.

When the taxi pulled up outside the Convent gate, Louis said – *Quick, man, quick. Drive on now. Get your foot down. To the house of Mr Monaghan. Surely he will know how we can enter the building.* That he said because Mr Monaghan was the Convent's farm steward and so was one of the few that came into those buildings.

But then it was that Mary Caffrey finally got the lock turned and the door of the Convent was opened. She waved her scattered arms then in the direction of the laundry but John McNally was having none of that. *Get the children out. Do you not see? The fire is spreading.* He spoke then to a nun but she said – *No, no, no.* He must go in the laundry first. He said then – *Give me the keys.* But she had not any keys.

John McNally looked up at the building, a place he had seen oft before through the windows of Sullivans, so he knew what a maze it was. A knot of staircases and corridors, inside and out, wooden and metal. How might you find your way in or out? Yet he could see the fire escape which was up on a wooden landing outside the upper dormitories.

Some others said to him – *We will try the fire escape, you see if the laundry door will give.* But a nun said – *No, no. Come down off there, it is the fire in the laundry which must be put out.* So then a group of them ran to the laundry door but it was still locked. The nuns said – *No, no, you must wait for the key.* But the men knew better and kicked it in.

Still the nuns did not want anyone up the fire escape but

Louis and Cissie went up anyway. Yet at the second floor they were stopped by a locked door into a classroom. Louis kicked at it, then tried to climb around it, but it would not give. They went back down to find something with which to break it in. All this was said later when the inquiry came.

While all this was passing, we girls were waiting in the Sacred Heart Dormitory, our hands knotted together, the little ones silent and hollow-eyed. Some stood up at the window, or sat on their beds, but some still had their heads under pillows, wanting to sleep. In that harsh and untimely light, it seemed that everything in that room sparkled and perhaps it did. For everything in that Convent shone, the floorboards, the iron beds, the wood of the cupboard doors, even the skirting boards and the ceilings themselves. We were clean girls.

When Miss O'Reilly came into the Sacred Heart Dormitory, she was not at all fussed. When she saw us at the window she said – *Stop that now. Get down on your knees and pray. Say an Act of Contrition.* Miss O'Reilly then crossed over into St Clare's. When she came back, she said – *You best go into the other dormitory until the door opens and things get fixed up.*

So we ran then into St Clare's pulling the little ones with us. The sound we made woke any there who were not yet out of bed. Yet we noticed even then how the girls got up, called out to ask what the disturbance was but then oft did sink back into bed, their heads being sent funny by the smoke, though you could see but little of it yet.

Some of us then crowded to the window of that dormitory. From there we saw the Garda and a group of others who seemed to be arguing over a mop. Some had gone into the infirmary and were carrying out the babies. Then the bottom door burst open, we heard the sound of it go, and girls started to pour out, their white nightdresses swelling as they ran, their hair long and straggling. They coughed and cried, stumbled, their eyes streaming, their hands gripped at their throats.

*

They said later that it was James Meehan, the taxi driver, who went to fetch the town's fire brigade. They came then with a hand cart and some lengths of hose which had been given to them by the water works caretaker. Yet at this time they still could not get into the courtyard as the gate was not unlocked, so they had to break the parlour window in the Convent and climb in that way. As they did so, others connected the hose to the stand pipe in the street. But soon it was found that the hoses were leaking so badly that, when the water was switched on, it could but dribble out.

*My sister, my sister. I must get her down.* That shout came from Kathleen, looking for Bernadette. Other voices came up from down the wooden stairs. Then banging and coughing, a sound of choking. But no one came up the stairs, only a wall of smoke. *We need a key for the fire escape. Where is the key?* Everywhere those words were being shouted as people fumbled and searched and questioned.

We need a gas mask. We'll not get through without. These voices we heard from the other side, where the door was, the way out to the fire escape, and a frantic banging as though someone was trying to break through a door with a stick. We said to each other – *We must pray. We must say an Act of Contrition.* But we could think of no prayers. *We need to have air. We need to have air.*

Then suddenly all was dark – not just our dormitory but the courtyard down below and all the Convent too. We heard then a door breaking somewhere close and a rush of air which pushed the smoke further upon us. Then another door opening and another rush of smoke. We were blown back into the room by the force of it. Girls tumbled and scrambled, arms and legs locked. *Oh Lord have mercy.*

Later John McNally and his friend from Fegans, John Paul Kennedy, told how they had got into the laundry and attacked the clothes drier – for that was the source of the fire, they thought.

When the extinguishers were emptied the men came out gasping for air. One of the nuns begged McNally – *Come now, like a good boy, go in and try again.* He asked for a wet cloth and Monaghan tied it around his nose and mouth. Armed again with fire extinguishers brought now from Sullivans store, he went back into the laundry where the wooden walls were crackling with flames. But McNally soon fell senseless and Kennedy dragged him out.

*Come out. Come out this way. The fire escape is open.* It was Mary Caffrey's voice. But we could not find the way for the smoke was curdling thick. Then Una Smith said to us – *What if there are still girls in Sacred Heart? How do we know that all came out?* So some went with her to check. With the tarry smoke and the solid dark, we could see naught. But we ran our hands over the beds, working down all the six rows.

So it was there we found Dolly Duffy, who was deaf. So we pulled her out. Then we were crossing back to St Clare's but we could not see the way. Then Una said – *It is this way. This way out.* But we said – *No, no.* For she was running into solid, gusting smoke. We called after her but it was too late and she had gone.

Dolly Duffy also said – *It is better this way. Down the wooden stairs. Come, come. We must run or we shall burn.* But we said – *No, no.* There is no way through. For we knew that all below was alight. But Dolly Duffy picked up an apron and wrapped it over her head. Then she rushed through an Act of Contrition and though we pleaded and pleaded with her to stay – yet she ran away from us down the wooden stairs.

Later it was the testimony of John McNally that, when he recovered consciousness, he asked – *The children are out, are they not? You have got the children out?* He was shouting it then at those who stood all about but no one wanted to reply. Until he shook Monaghan by the collar. *No, no*, Monaghan said. *The children are up there. Here take the keys. See what you may do. Blessed Mary have mercy on us.*

So McNally went up the iron staircase but the smoke was too dense. It was just as he turned to come down that he saw a girl burst out of the other door, and the soles of her feet were burning. She ran screaming across the courtyard, her arms waving, her eyes rolling. Screaming and screaming, her feet blazing fire.

Forty feet up to our dormitory. We knew we were trapped. And yet we said – *Get the youngest children out. That's what we must do.* So we pushed them ahead of us towards the closed door. Then we pulled it open but so strangling and grasping were the fumes which burst in, that we could only push it shut again, our eyes stinging and swollen.

We tried then to get to the window, crawling over beds or under them, keeping low to the floor. Until we were looking down into the courtyard. Down below all was chaos and commotion, with many people running to and fro. We heard them shout that the ladders were coming. We opened the windows and bashed on the sections which did not give. Some of us sat on the beds and gathered the smaller children around us. We began to lead them in a decade of the rosary. *Hail Mary, full of Grace, the Lord is with thee. Pray for us sinners now and at the hour of our death.*

Those down below knew that ladders were then the only hope. So they ran through the unlit streets to the market yard where they knew the town council kept ladders, and tried to raise the caretaker. He had no bell to his quarters but after much yelling and bashing a window opened. The caretaker was angry to be woken, so flung the keys down and they were lost in the dark.

Louis Blessing then had found a bicycle and pedalled furiously up to the Central Hotel where he and several other bachelors in the town had rooms. He burst into the room of Mattie Hand, shouting and roaring. Grabbing hold of Mattie's shoulder, he pulled him from the bed. Mattie saying – *Louis, what are you doing, you blessed fool?* For he thought this was some jest.

But soon enough he understood for Mattie Hands worked with the Electricity Supply Board and had ladders in the back of his van. While Mattie dressed, Louis cycled back to the market yard where he found people still stumbling around trying to find the key. But it was hopeless in the dark, so they smashed open a door, and finally the ladders were located and the men seized them and ran to Sullivans yard.

On the way they met a squad of soldiers brought out of the town barracks and now quick-marching in formation up the main street. Coming into the courtyard the men with ladders and the soldiers found a crowd gripped by panic. Sparks, fireballs and pieces of slate were raining down. Flames and smoke billowed out of every window.

The three top windows were crowded with a sea of childish faces. Screaming, praying, coughing, calling out – *Get us out, we are smothering.* Then a girl jumped, rising up first, so it seemed, like some great white bird, then dipping down, falling faster and faster through the air. Even the blankets spread out below could not break her fall.

We were trying to say the rosary again. Dear Lord, we were trying. But the little children were all screaming. Once again some of us went to the door and tried to open it but we were suffocated by smoke. Mary Lowry, with her gold chain still around her neck, dropped to the floor. Kathleen crawled under the beds to the window.

When we were halfway through the third decade of the rosary, we could go no further. So we joined those others then at the window. I am sorry to say that we were treading on the younger children who were down below and had been knocked senseless by the fumes. We could not do otherwise as we must have air.

We saw down below poor Maureen who had jumped and Miss Harrington standing near her. But Miss Harrington never went to pick her up. It was Dolly Duffy, though her feet were burnt black, she was the one as went to pick up poor broken Maureen.

Then we saw men putting up a ladder against the wall but it fell short of the window. *Look, look. See it does not reach. How will we get down?* Back again then to the door to make one last attempt to get out that way but now flames poured in and we could not get the door shut again such was the force of the blast.

Below we saw the men, and the soldiers also, struggling to extend the ladders. One went up partially but did not reach our window and came off the pulleys. The other had ropes tied around it. The men got them untangled but still it would not extend. So they lashed the two pieces together but, as it went up, it soon swayed and fell apart.

We heard then a rush and crash as the wooden stairs below us collapsed. The men were calling up then, telling us to jump. We said – *No, no.* For it was too far down. But still another did jump. A man tried his best to hold her but she too crashed down, smashing her legs. To one side there was a lean-to shed and one girl tried also to jump onto there but she bounced off and hit the ground. After that none of us wanted to jump.

We saw men place a section of the council ladder on the roof of the lean-to shed. One man then came up and stood up close to the window. *Come on, girl. Come on. Jump. Jump.* So one did, then another and another. But when the fourth jumped the man lost his balance. He and the child fell on the shed roof and the ladder crashed to the ground.

The window then was burning hot. The glass cracking, blowing out, melting down. The floor started to go. Wardrobes and beds disappeared into the furnace. One girl was lying unconscious on her bed, the clothes on her back on fire. Then she disappeared. The two Carrolls were calling for each other and the McKiernans, hollering and spluttering, arms outstretched.

Then the floor where they were disappeared. Only those of us on the windowsill now were left.

Praise God a man came with a better ladder, got it extended in seconds. But though we were throat-raw and suffocated, we were afeard to go. He put out his hands and pulled some of us off, placing us on the ladder so that we might get down. But when it came to the turn of Bernadette, who was but seven years old, she tried to go back into the room, such was her terror.

Theresa it was went after her and tried to catch hold of her. But Bernadette still was wriggling away back into the flames, though only a tiny patch of floor was left. So Theresa then got hold of her by the hair, pulled her towards the window, dragged her hand towards the man on the ladder so that he then got her down. Though by then Bernadette's back and hair were all flaming alight.

At the inquiry it was explained that it was Mattie Hands who finally got the ladders up. Also Dr John Sullivan, brother of those Sullivans who owned the store. When he got abreast of the window it was pumping tarry smoke. He had only time to look through for one moment. A heap of children was struggling about the level of the window. Cries were still coming there.

But he could not breathe and came a step or two down the ladder, putting his head under the windowsill where the air was clearer. As he hung there, he heard still the groans and cries from within. Again he pulled his head over the sill but he could see little and the smoke was making him weak. *I would have done anything on this earth to get in but I could not do it.*

As he came down the ladder, flames smashed out through the window above. A roar, a heaving, a smash of timbers. Another as the roof blew right into the night. He called and called then, shouting until his voice was hoarse, but no voice from the window echoed back to him. The time was 2.40 a.m.

*

The next day the orphanage was nothing but a burnt-out frame, with damp wisps of smoke curling out through the debris. Only the many iron beds could you see still standing, stuck up in curved shapes, like the ribcages of so many skeleton beasts. And a pile of hoops lying in the yard. All the businesses premises in the town were closed and a sickening smell spread all about.

Matt McKiernan, the brother of Mary and Susan, who lived twelve miles from Cavan, was told of the fire that morning and pedalled furiously to Butlersbridge where he went to the Post Office and called to the Garda who told him then that his sisters were dead. Although it was Lent at that time, and many were on the tack, yet they did take to the liquor that day.

It was not until darkness was falling that all the bodies were brought out. Then the men shouldered the coffins and took them to the Convent chapel, laid them down near the altar. Over the days that followed donations flooded in to the Bishop and the Abbess from all around.

Yet no one thought to get a call through to Matt McKiernan and his brother Hugh, who had lost their two sisters. So when the family came into the town to the funeral, the procession had already gone out to Cullies Graveyard. But Mrs Carroll, who had lost two daughters, now she *was* at the funeral, gripping the hand of her surviving daughter, whom she had dressed in a scarlet coat. *I'll never step into a Catholic church again as long as I live.*

Later we were asked – those of us who still had tongues to speak – about what happened. For an inquiry was established by Judge McCarthy, sent up from Dublin. You must say your age and your work within the orphanage. Cook, portress, maid, needleworker or laundress. Even though you fainted you must go back the next day. Though at least for the inquiry no one had to walk out in two left boots, as was often the way. Just as we had learnt the catechism, so the nuns taught us what we must say.

It was said – *Of course, many of those orphan girls are simple.* But we were not simple, we were frightened. Nuns with the rosary on their wrist, the cane hanging next to it. Mother Carmel would strip your clothes from your body, beat you skinless. We were asked again and again – *You knew the instructions in case of a fire so why did you not follow those procedures?* Yet that question was never asked of the nuns.

It was a pitiful business when all was told. That was widely agreed. It was said in the town – *The brigade were not fit to wash a bus.* It was also said privately – *Course the building burnt so fast due to all that floor polish.* Yet the Council were able to reassure the inquiry that faulty equipment had played no part. The ladders and hoses were all in excellent order.

Questions were asked about the fire escape. It was but seven foot away from the dormitory so why were the children not able to get out? And the lights in the building – why were they switched off? Miss O'Reilly was questioned at some length. *Was there not a full fifteen minutes during which those children could have been brought down?*

Miss O'Reilly could not say, the questioning made her confused. She was also the sister of the Mother Abbess and so must be treated with respect. *Which nun was it who had tried to prevent the men from going up the fire escape? No, no. That was not what happened.* The question could not be pursued.

Nor was it asked why some of those girls were ever in the orphanage. For many were not orphans. Susan and Mary McKiernan had brothers and a father. But after their mother died they were sent to the orphanage. A neighbour offered to take them but that woman was a Protestant so she was not allowed.

Yet, in truth, you could not blame the nuns. Sure they took those children in and the state gave them no money for it. They were good women who did their best. Yet still in the town it was whispered – *It was because those girls must not be seen in their nightdresses by the men of the town.*

＊

We are the children of Cavan. Have you heard speak of us? From all around they saw us burn but none could help. Now and in the hour of our death. Sure it was discipline and fear which killed us, not the wire in the laundry clothes drier. We are still waiting at the window. And Louis Blessing is still bashing at the fire escape with a mop. And Matt McKiernan is still riding his bike to Butlersbridge and to the phone call that will stake his heart.

John McNally, please please will you bring the ladder up to us? Or must we run to heaven with our feet on fire? They put on our gravestone – *Children pray for us*. Thirty-five girls but only eight coffins. It was only Mary Lowry they could identify – her with the gold cross she had from the Bishop. All of the nuns safe enough, so God be praised. Many years have passed now. It was long ago. But we are still waiting. Please – will you not put up the ladders and bring us down?

This story is based on documents and personal testimony relating to the fire at St Joseph's orphanage in Cavan on the night of 23 February 1943.

# Acknowledgements

These stories originally appeared in the following collections and publications.

'The Stop' in *The Yellow Room*, 2009.

'Ray the Rottweiler' in *Prospect* and *RSL Review*, 2015.

'The Last House on the Marsh' in *Manchester Review*, 2019.

'From Far Around They Saw Us Burn' in *Ploughshares* (March 2020), *The Best Short Stories 2021: The O. Henry Prize Winners* (Anchor Books, 2021) and *The Best British Short Stories 2021* (Salt, 2021).

'All the Places that I Have Not Seen' in *Riptide*, 2020.

'We All Know Mr Jones' in *Moxy*, 2020.

'Safe Passage' in *Southword*, 2021.

Many thanks to all of these magazines and publishers and also to the short story awards who have recognised my work: the Fish Short Story Prize, the Galley Beggar Press Short Story Prize, the Colm Toíbín International Short Story Award (organised by Wexford Literary Festival), the Bare Fiction Short Story Prize and the V. S. Pritchett Memorial Prize (organised by the Royal Society of Literature).

Thanks to Merric Davidson who was an early supporter of my short stories and also to Ladette Randolph, editor-in-chief of *Ploughshares*, and Jenny Minton Quigley of the O. Henry

Prize. Also, Nicholas Royle and Salt Publishing, John Holland of Stroud Short Stories and Caroline Sanderson of *The Bookseller* and Stroud Book Festival.

Writing friends have also read, commented and edited. Thanks to Susannah Rickards, Rebecca Abrams, Sally Bayley, Clare Andrews, Roopa Farooki and Clare Morgan. A massive thank you to John Mitchinson, Rachael Kerr, Rina Gill, Alex Eccles, Imogen Denny, Lisa Fiske and all the team at Unbound. Also, thanks to Tamsin Shelton for copy-editing.

I am hugely grateful to my agent Victoria Hobbs at A. M. Heath and I send love and thanks, as always, to Stephen, Thomas and Hope Kinsella. Last, and perhaps most importantly, my thanks to all the friends, family and supporters who have pledged for this book. Your generosity and enthusiasm make it possible for me to keep writing.

# A Note on the Author

Alice Jolly is a novelist and playwright. She won the 2014 V. S. Pritchett Memorial Prize with one of her short stories, 'Ray the Rottweiler', and her memoir *Dead Babies and Seaside Towns* won the 2016 PEN Ackerley Prize. She has published two novels with Simon & Schuster – *What the Eye Doesn't See* and *If Only You Knew* – and four of her plays have been produced by the professional company of the Everyman Theatre in Cheltenham. Her novel *Mary Ann Sate, Imbecile*, published by Unbound in 2018, was longlisted for the RSL Ondaatje Prize and shortlisted for the Rathbones Folio Prize. Her latest novel, *Between the Regions of Kindness*, was published by Unbound in 2019. In 2021, Jolly was awarded an O. Henry Prize for her short story 'From Far Around They Saw Us Burn'. She lives in Stroud, Gloucestershire.

Unbound is the world's first crowdfunding publisher, established in 2011.

We believe that wonderful things can happen when you clear a path for people who share a passion. That's why we've built a platform that brings together readers and authors to crowdfund books they believe in – and give fresh ideas that don't fit the traditional mould the chance they deserve.

This book is in your hands because readers made it possible. Everyone who pledged their support is listed below. Join them by visiting unbound.com and supporting a book today.

Rebecca Abrams

Clare Andrews

David Baillie

Jason Ballinger

Chris Blackhurst

Georgina Blastland

Graham Blenkin

Denise Boggs

Mark Bowsher

John Boyce

Stephanie Bretherton

Alexander Brostoff

Sarah Jane Brostoff

Kate Calico

Alistair Canlin

Louise Cartledge

Andy Charman

Norma Clarke

Vanessa Cobb

Jude Cook

Tina Cowen

Judith and Geoff Dance

Sara Davies

Philip de Jersey

Micheline Decker

Mike Dickson

Maura Dooley

Jane Draycott

Lily Dunn

Gillian Eastwood

Frank Egerton

Jess Egerton

Ashley Elliott

Jude Emmet

Lara Feigel

Daisy Finer

Paul Garner

Matt Gibson

Tom Gillingwater

Guinevere Glasfurd

Sarah Goldson

David Graham

Anthony A. Gribben

Lindis Harris

David Hebblethwaite

Amanda Holmes Duffy

Katie Jarvis

Dan Jenkins

Beverley Johnson

Kathleen Jones

Sean Jones

Olivia Katrandjian

Val Kemp

Dan Kieran

Michael Kingston

Angela Kinsella

Tony Kinsella

Bronia Kita

Tara Kunert

Laura Kinsella Foundation

Elizabeth Loudon

Sally Lovell

Alison MacLeod

Jane Malcolm

Rachel Malik

Bee Martin

Maya Matthews

Yvonne Carol McCombie

Megan McCormick

David McMahon

Iain McNicol

David Melvin

Martin Mills and Sarah Pickstone

John Mitchinson

Blake Morrison

Emma Mosley

Carlo Navato

Ravi Nayer

Kristina Nordlander

Jennie Pears

Esme Podmore

Justin Pollard

Katharine Quarmby

Robert Randall

Fergus Randolph

Sam Reese

Annabel Richmond

Susannah Rickards

Jane Rogers

Lorraine Rogerson

Jonathan Ruppin

Caroline Sanderson

Cherise Saywell

Antonio Seghesio

Katri Skala

Sam Henley Smith

Zoe Somerville

Richard Stein

Gillian Stern

Catherine Stewart

Philip Stewart

Alan Teder

Lynda Mia Thompson

Ann Tudor

Mark Vent

Valeria Vescina

Miranda Williams